The Werewolves of Green Lake

The Monsters of Green Lake, Volume 1

C. Dennis Moore

Published by Shrine Keepers Publishing, 2015.

Also by C. Dennis Moore

an Angel Hill short
Carlotta Valdez
Flagpole Sitta
Woolly Muffler
Private Helicopter
Problems and Bigger Ones
Jack the Lion
Old Hat
Terminal Annex
Wrecking Ball

Holiday Horrors
New Year's Day
Martin Luther King, Jr. Day
Groundhog Day
Ash Wednesday
Valentine's Day
Presidents' Day
Saint Patrick's Day

LATE-NIGHT DOUBLE FEATURES
Playground of the Gods
House of Limbs

Mini Collections
Five Fates
Five Fantasies
Five Furies

standalone shorts
Coming Down the Mountain
Revenge of the Roach King
Maggie Andrews Gets the Facts
Blood Bitch
Son of Man
The Legend of Mr. Cairo
Plaything
Illusion is a Synonym for Dream
Raw Materials
The Caterpillar
In the Town of Broken Dreams
Working for the Fat Man
The League of Liars
Biscuithead
The Fish in the Fields

The Envy of Falling Leaves
Road to Nowhere
The Timesmiths

The Angel Hill novels
The Man in the Window
The Ghosts of Mertland
The Flip
Housequake
The Third Floor 2: Suicide House
The Third Floor

The Monsters of Green Lake
The Werewolves of Green Lake
The Vampires of Green Lake
The Witches of Green Lake
The Demons of Green Lake

Writers' Library
10 Writing Prompts That Work (and the stories to prove it)
Doing it Write
Writing Rules
Shut Up and Write

Standalone
Aftermath
Terrible Thrills
Bloodletting
Dancing on a Razorblade
The Dichotomy of Monsters
Love Jones
What the Blind Man Saw
Camdigan
Kung Fu Sasquatch
Science Fiction Double Feature (Foodies of Mars variant)
Science Fiction Double Feature (Purple Haze variant)
So Quake With Fear, You Tiny Fools!
The Nightmare Corridor
The Only Way Out is Through
The Organ Grinder
Revelations
Alter
The Lonely Man: Road to The Third Floor 2
Red House
Fluke
The American Way Vs. Dr. Brain
Welcome to the Trust

Acknowledgments:

Cover photo courtesy of breakermaximus

FRIDAY

• • • •

THE WIND WHIPPED PAST HIS FACE and through the scruff of closely-cropped dark hair as the world turned upside down, rushing blood briefly to David Reed's head before turning right side up again. He closed his eyes to the flashing colored lights and wished he could do the same against the shrill screams of teenage girls—two of whom belonged to his own daughters Victoria and Alison—and he felt a rumble in his stomach that he knew immediately was bad news.

He wondered when the ride would end, hoped it would be soon, then hoped even stronger that he could hold down that churning until then. When the ride finally began to slow, it seemed the urge to vomit grew even stronger, to be free of the harness, out of the cage, and off the platform an immediate, driving need.

His heart pounded and sweat beaded on his forehead as he waited for the carnie to unlock the ride and let everyone out.

As soon as he heard the click releasing the catch on the lock, he threw off the seatbelt and leapt out of the seat, climbed over his younger daughter Alison, and darted down the stairs to dash behind a pillar and vomit.

Overhead, cars roared past on the highway, under which the fall carnival had been set up. The sound soothed his mind, but his stomach was still a roiling pot of rotten stew and boiling acid. He heaved and spewed more pizza, which had obviously been a terrible idea right before the Tilt-A-Whirl and the Chicago Loop. He'd thought his stomach stronger, but then he reminded himself he wasn't twenty anymore. The stomach of a forty-five-year-old was made of much weaker stuff, apparently.

He closed his eyes and let the breeze fill his lungs while the whoosh of the cars above his head made him think of a relaxing beach.

Calm down, he told his body. No more vomiting. He caught a whiff of funnel cake in the air and the sweet stench of it assaulted him, threatening a new barrage.

The sweat on his back and neck chilled him when the wind blew by and he shivered, which only made him want to throw up again. He knelt on one knee, then leaned forward and squeezed his eyes shut, drawing himself as much into a ball as he could without lying on the cracked concrete.

When the moment had passed, he stood up, took a deep breath and shook off the nausea. The speakers set up around the park blasted old rock music. He looked around for his wife and daughters. He spotted Jessi, her short frame topped with curly auburn locks, a little distance away. The girls, Victoria having inherited her mother's hair color while Alison, a year younger, had David's black hair, were watching the next ride in line with wide and eager eyes. Jessi watched David with concern, and a little bit of "I told you not to eat so much before we came". But mostly concern. Or so he chose to believe.

"Are you ready yet, Dad?" Alison asked, barely able to stop herself from running toward the next ride, which was currently unloading its previous round of riders.

"Go on without me," David said, waving them off. The girls both smiled and took off.

"I told you not to eat so much before we came," Jessi said as he sidled up next to her.

"Yeah," he agreed. "I think they purposely make those things fast and jerky like that."

"Of course they do," Jessi said with authority, as if she'd just read the statistics.

"Well, it's a stupid practice. You want people to enjoy the rides and come back."

Jessi had no comment.

He watched Victoria and Alison climb aboard the next ride, one of David's favorites growing up, the Octopus, knowing there was no way his stomach could have handled even that junior league contraption.

It would have to be enough, this time, just to watch his daughters enjoy it. Jessi hadn't gone near a ride all evening, even though David had sprung for free access bracelets for all four of them. She hated the sensation, but didn't seem to mind watching everyone else having a good time. David, on the other hand, envied his daughters their stronger stomachs, although he realized he was only going to be able to watch for a few seconds. When their car took its first dip and spin, his stomach gave a warning grumble and he had to look away.

He tried to look distracted or disinterested, but feared it only came across as weak, so he peeked back at them, saw the smiles on their faces, and wanted to watch. But his stomach gave that warning again and David looked behind him, watching the carnies work.

He wondered what kind of life they led when they weren't out here running these rickety machines. He thought about when he and the Bewlay boys used to come here in high school, and how grungy the workers always looked.

"I'm not getting on that thing," Mick Bewlay said once, regarding the filthy toothless man running the Himalaya. "He couldn't bother to brush, I'm supposed to trust him to tighten all the nuts and bolts on that deathtrap?"

"Don't be a wuss," Mick's brother Donny had said. They were fraternal twins who went to great lengths to look more like each other. Both kept their hair long and wore matching denim jackets which, later in life, would become denim vests over black motorcycle tees. David remembered they had tried to grow beards that year. Donnie had managed it just fine, but Mick's had come in patchy and haphazard, leaving Donnie to mock him until he gave in and shaved it off. "He didn't build the thing, he just pushes the button. Get on."

And they had all made it off the ride safe and sound, if a little sore in the shoulder and chest muscles from the centrifugal force.

And now look at me, David thought. I eat a few slices of pizza and I can't handle a couple of loops. Pathetic. The Bewlays would never let me live this down.

He glanced back at the ride again and knew that was it for him tonight. As soon as it was over, he gathered his daughters and said, "Alright, you two, I think it's time to head home."

They gave disappointed groans and Jessi said, "You'll be alright," as they ushered the girls toward the parking lot.

"I gotta work tomorrow, anyway," David said.

"You mean you don't want to make us watch you throw up again," Victoria said.

"That too," David agreed.

His head pounded now and he felt a moment of dread at the thought of lying in bed and closing his eyes, worried it would be the same effect as if he'd had too much to drink. Right now, a spinning room was the last thing he needed. But the second to last thing he needed was to stand around here anymore with all these lights flashing, with the blaring music was half a dozen sets of speakers placed around the park, all blasting different tunes. He'd rather lose himself in the calm of the cars rushing overhead.

"Maybe we'll come back later in the week, before they leave town," David suggested. The girls smiled and said, "Fine," and followed their parents to the car.

"He said maybe," Jessi clarified. "These carnivals aren't cheap."

"We'll figure it out," David said more to his daughters than his wife. They knew that meant he'd have to ask again later when their mother was in a good mood.

Alison slid in first, and Victoria barked, "Watch the bow!"

Jessi looked back and said, "I thought I told you to take that stuff inside?"

"I will!" Victoria said. "Jeez!" She held out her hands and Alison handed over Victoria's bow. "Will you hand me the glove too, please?"

Alison looked around, then spotted it on the floor, bent to grab it, and handed it to her sister.

"Thank you," Victoria said and Jessi nodded in appreciation from the front seat.

Only a year apart, the girls could never decide if they were friends or enemies. It seemed the competitions never ended. If one decided she wanted to take swimming, the other decided archery was the thing for her. If one got all As on her grade card, the other tried for A+s. Perfect attendance was never a problem, because there was an award for that at the end of the year, and one of them was not going to let the other win if they didn't themselves.

But David had to admit, driving home that night, glad to be away from the noise and chaos, when it really came down to it, the girls had each other's backs no matter what. That always made him feel like, despite the constant civil war waging between Alison and Victoria, somewhere along the way he and Jessi had managed to do something right.

He watched the moving lights fade in the mirror as he drove home.

. . . .

THE NEXT AFTERNOON, David sat in the break room at Cleo's Market in town, reading a copy of Elmore Leonard's *52 Pick-Up* and drinking a Vanilla Coke. He only had twenty pages left and wanted to finish it, which was exactly why, he assumed, Beth Gilmore decided to sit next to him and start talking.

"What are you doing, Mr. Reed?"

What the hell does it look like, he wanted to ask.

Instead he said, "I'm not your teacher anymore, Beth, you can call me David now."

"Nah," she said. "Too weird. What are you reading?"

He tilted the paperback toward himself so she could see the cover.

"Wasn't that a movie?"

"It was," he replied, never taking his eyes from the page and hoping she would take the hint.

"You sure like to read," she said.

You mean I *would* like to read, he thought.

Instead he said, "Uh huh," again hoping she would take the hint.

"I can never concentrate enough, I guess I just have too much going on in my head."

I doubt that's it, he thought.

Instead he said, "Uh huh," still hoping she would take the hint.

"Maybe I just have to find the right book."

He replaced his bookmark and set the book down in surrender.

Instead he decided to go on the offensive.

"Why are you still here, Beth?" he asked. "I mean here, working here. You worked here when you were in high school. You graduated a few years ago. Isn't there something else you'd rather be doing with your life?"

"You work here," she said. "And you're older than I am."

That didn't work, he thought.

"Yeah well, I also have a mortgage and a family to raise."

"Doesn't your wife work at St. Vincent's over in West?" Beth asked.

David nodded, knowing what she was getting at. And while he'd always just been glad of Jessi's help with the bills—God knew teaching basic math to a bunch of unresponsive high school students at Green Lake High didn't cover what the Reeds needed to survive—there was a secret part of him that he never let be seen in public that resented her good fortune.

He knew he was too mature to get bogged down in that macho alpha male bullshit where he had to be the breadwinner, but that secret part of him would probably always hate the fact Jessi made more than he did, and she only had to work one job to do it. It didn't help he was teaching in public school while Jessi taught Sociology in a private school across the river, a position that allowed them to get their girls in at a discounted tuition. And, yes, he was thankful for that, too, but it wasn't *him* who had done it. And, sure, there were times when he wondered what made Jessi so special she got the sweet gig while he was, let's face it, slumming it.

"And let that be a lesson to you," he said, getting up with his book and his bottle.

"What lesson would that be?"

"I'll get back to you on that one," he said. "My break's over."

It wasn't, but this conversation was going nowhere except down a road he didn't want to go down with a former student, especially Beth Gilmore who apparently still hadn't gotten over failing David's class her Junior year. Apparently she would always put that on him instead of admitting if she'd just bothered to come to class once in a while she might have squeaked by with a D. Apparently she was going to use every opportunity she got to dig at David and make him feel like a failure at life.

I don't need that shit, he thought, and disappeared into the bathroom.

When he came out, he finished off the Coke, tossed the bottle into the trash, and slid his book into his back pocket, then went back to work.

He spent the last two hours in the dairy cooler stocking milk and trying to clean up his area so it wasn't so impossible to move around in there. He knew there was a truck due tonight, and with his luck it would be there before his shift was up. The last thing he wanted tonight was to have to squeeze in half a dozen pallets where they wouldn't fit.

As luck would have it, for a change, the truck still hadn't arrived by the time David clocked out that night.

Before going home, he did the week's grocery shopping, then loaded the bags into the back of his '05 Outback—a car he wished he had the money to replace—then drove home.

The Reeds lived off a stretch of road more commonly known in town as the "back road", but which was, in fact, unmarked and didn't appear on any maps. Mail was delivered to a box in front of his house marked simply Box 34, and if they wanted a pizza delivered, they just told the driver "it's on the back road, about five miles in from town," and that was good enough.

David had made it halfway home that night, the moon guiding him, when his thoughts strayed to Ashley, a girl he worked with. She was way too young for him, and totally not interested, but David sometimes had a hard time not staring and showing his interest too overtly. As much as he needed this job, the last thing he wanted to do was make it awkward. But that didn't stop his mind from wandering in his off time.

Currently, he was blasting a David Bowie album and imagining Ashley in the seat next to him. Bowie was well before her time, but he imagined she was hip enough she'd dig the hell out of it if he introduced her to it (after all, the first time he saw her, she'd been wearing a Doctor Who shirt with BAD WOLF across the front), and they could bond over the music, then they could move on to sharing their interests in books, movies, and soon each other.

It would be a good life, he thought. He'd be happy and wake up each morning to a day full of possibility.

That wasn't to say he was unhappy at home, necessarily. David loved Jessi. They had built a real life together—more real and comfortable than anything he could ever have with Ashley. Ashley was a fantasy, and he knew it. But sometimes it was good to retreat into fantasy, just for a minute. But at the end of the day, he knew he wasn't going anywhere. Ashley was unpredictable, she was unsafe. Jessi was easy.

Damn, Ashley had a set of tits on her that wouldn't quit, though. And what a smile.

And that was as far as he got in his musings because his lack of focus meant he didn't see the hulking shape in the middle of the back road until he was almost on it. Luckily, his reflexes kicked in and David yanked the wheel to the right, swerved only inches from clipping the thing in the road, bounced over a dip in the gravel and careened into a ditch. The Outback was airborne for a second, then came to rest with a crunch of the hood smack into a utility pole, knocking David's head into the steering wheel. He came up dazed, dizzy, and with a throbbing pain right in the center of his head.

He tried to blink away the pain, then looked around, wondering if he'd killed whatever he hit, then remembering he hadn't hit it. At least, he didn't think he had.

His phone had been knocked from the dock in the impact, silencing the music.

David did a quick check of himself, concentrating on any pain he might have. It didn't feel like anything was broken, and the only thing that really hurt was his forehead.

The seatbelt had done its job, while the airbag had not, but he seemed no worse for the wear, so he'd overlook it for now and write a strongly-worded email to the company later. Maybe.

For now he had to get the groceries home and see what the damage to his car was, probably in that order.

He tried to start it, but knew immediately that option was out. He looked out the cracked windshield and tried to gauge the damage, but wasn't able to get a good look from inside. He'd have to get out. He tried the door. The handle released and the door opened with a faint click. But something stopped David's hand.

What had he almost hit?

It had been big, whatever it was. In fact, it had been huge. Like man-height. But, while he'd only gotten the briefest, vaguest look at it, he knew it was no man. Just then, he heard something move outside the car.

He didn't look. He suddenly didn't care what he'd almost hit. In fact, if it moved away and the dread he felt rising drained away, he'd just call them even and they could go back to their own lives. He couldn't say why he felt this way, why there was such an intense feeling of doom suddenly looming over him, but it was there, and he knew if he turned and acknowledged whatever was outside his car, it would only make things worse.

Instead, he pulled the door closed again, locked it, and kept his eyes forward.

He felt it moving closer. He heard it growling. A smell like old socks soaked in curdled milk seeped into the car.

He knew black bears were native to Missouri, but he was pretty sure they'd been nearly wiped out of the area. Maybe not all of them, though.

He wished he was one of those people who carry guns in their car. A shotgun, he thought. That's what he needed. He sat frozen, expecting any second for a huge paw to come crashing through the window and haul him outside where he'd be mauled to death.

The growling moved closer.

He wondered if he could lay on the horn and scare it away, or if the noise would just make it angry.

Then it didn't matter, because a pair of headlights appeared in the distance, coming toward him, and he heard whatever was outside scurry off.

As the headlights grew closer, David finally looked around to make sure he was alone. The fields spreading out to the left were empty. Whatever had been there was fast.

The car coming down the back road slowed when they saw David's crumpled mess and he saw it was Parker Newsome who lived further down the road.

Parker pulled his pick-up to the side of the road, got out and came over to David's door.

"You okay, Mr. Reed?"

"Yeah," David said, opening the door. "I think so anyway."

"Dude, this car is totaled!" Parker said, sounding like he was trying to hold in his laughter.

"Yeah," David said again. "I need to call and get it towed. You think you could give me a ride up to the house? I've got groceries in the back."

"No problem," Parker said. "How'd you wind up over there, anyway? You been drinking?"

David shook his head and said, "Something in the road, came out of nowhere. Did you see anything run off when you were driving up here?"

Parker looked around.

"I don't see anything."

"No, it's gone, whatever it was. Ran off when you showed up."

"Oh," Parker said. "I didn't see it."

"That's okay," David said, sure that whatever it was had been good and frightened and wouldn't be back. "Can you help me get these bags?"

"Sure."

They transferred David's groceries to the back of Parker's truck, then David called Sandy Miller who had the only tow truck in town, told him where he'd wrecked, and asked him to take the Outback back to Sandy's shop. Sandy agreed and David thanked him, then asked how much for the tow?

"Fifty for the tow," Sandy said, "but I can't say how much to fix it."

"That's alright," David said. "We'll worry about that tomorrow or something. I'll leave sixty under the floor mat, okay?"

Sandy agreed with a hearty, "Sure thing," and David felt a stab in his chest when he pulled those three twenties from his wallet, knowing that, no matter how much the repairs were, that ten in change would never be seen again. And now he was going to have to go to the ATM tomorrow because those twenties had been for the girls' lunches at school. Unfortunately, discounted tuition didn't mean discounted lunches, and somehow it had worked out that, since Jessi drove them to school, David got to pay for lunch. He wasn't sure how that balanced out at all since Jessi was going there every day anyway, but he just kept his mouth shut and avoided the unwinnable argument.

Parker dropped him off at home and helped him carry the groceries inside, and David tried to slip him a ten, all he had left in his wallet, but Parker just waved it off and said, "No problem, Mr. Reed. Glad I could help."

What he meant was Glad I could come inside and get a peek at your daughter, whom Parker had carried a not-so-secret crush over for several years. David thanked God Victoria either hadn't noticed or had noticed and determined Parker wasn't her type. Daughters on Dates was one of the things he was hoping to avoid as long as possible.

"Why is Parker helping you carry in groceries?" Jessi asked after the boy had left.

"Same reason I'm gonna need to use your car to go to work tomorrow," David said. "Something ran in front of me on the road and when I swerved to miss it, I hit a pole instead. Sandy's gonna tow it in for me."

"Did you total it?"

"Not sure. I hope not, but it was bad enough I couldn't drive it away from there."

"Then you totaled it," Jessi said.

"Not necessarily. We'll see what Sandy says tomorrow after he has a chance to look at it."

"What was in the middle of the road?"

"I have no idea," David said, unloading a bag full of canned soups and setting them on the counter before moving them to the pantry. "Something big."

"Were you texting and driving?"

"I was driving," he said. "That's it."

"And you didn't see something standing in the middle of the road? You must have been texting."

"I wasn't texting. It ran out in front of me and I reacted."

He unloaded a few frozen pizzas, then started rearranging the contents of the freezer to make them fit.

"You need to just quit that job so you're not driving at night, anyway. You know you can't see shit at night."

"When I get a raise at the school, I'll quit. Or we could sell the house and rent someplace smaller."

"I'm not living in town," Jessi said.

"Then I'm working two jobs," David said. "Have to, you know that."

She rolled her eyes and walked out, claiming a headache, leaving David to put the groceries away by himself.

Seriously, though, he wondered. How did he not see that thing in the road? Had it really run out in front of him? He had been thinking about Ashley, imagining her in the seat beside him, singing along to "Drive-In Saturday", but his eyes had still been on the road. And he'd driven the back road enough times he noticed when one of the roadside trees had been pruned by the city. But he hadn't seen something as big as that thing had been until it was right in front of him?

Maybe Jessi was right, and he really couldn't see at night. He may need glasses. But first thing was first: he had to get his car fixed before he did anything. With both of them working at the same time, and in opposite directions, it wasn't going to be long before she was tired of leaving extra early to take him to work and then having to pick him up in the evenings.

He really didn't think it had been a bear, that had only been his initial adrenaline-fueled imagining. He'd lived his forty-five years in Green Lake and had never seen a bear. So what the hell was it?

That growling, it sounded like a dog. But he'd never seen a dog that big. Nor did he ever want to.

SUNDAY

· · · ·

BEFORE LEAVING FOR his shift at Cleo's the next afternoon, David called Sandy Miller to ask about his Outback.

"Well, you've got two options, way I see it," Sandy said.

"Can it be fixed?" David asked.

"That's one of the options," Sandy said. "I was getting to that. You can fix it. But if you want my professional opinion, it would be cheaper to scrap it, sell it for parts. You really messed it up, Mr. Reed."

David groaned.

"How much to fix it?" he asked.

Sandy rattled a quote off the top of his head and David said, "Shit, my first car didn't cost that much."

"Yeah," Sandy said.

"How much would I get if I sold it for parts, do you think?"

"Depends. I mean, you can say you're selling it, but if no one's buying, no one's buying."

"Can we sell it for scrap?"

"If you want to," Sandy said. "Can't promise you'd get much, just if you want my honest opinion."

David had long believed when someone said "If you want my honest opinion", their *honest* opinion was the last thing you were getting. He had a feeling Sandy, as the only mechanic in Green Lake, had the contacts to get a good amount out of the Outback. Only he'd try to pocket the bulk of that if he could.

"Alright," David said. "Thanks, I've got to get to work, but I'll figure out what I want to do and call you back maybe tomorrow or something, okay?"

"No problem, Mr. Reed," Sandy said. "Just know I can't keep it sitting here for too long. This isn't the junk yard.'

"I know, I'll get it out of your way, promise." He hung up, then spent half an hour trying to get Jessi to just take him in and drop him off, but she told him, "I'm not up to it. Go ahead and take the Rover."

Whatever, he decided, knowing time was running out and he didn't have all day to go round and round with her over it. On the drive there, his thoughts began to drift to Ashley again, until he reached the pole he'd hit last night.

He pulled over and looked at the spot where his car had come to rest. Broken glass from one of his headlights lay in the grass. He looked in the road for tracks, thinking maybe he could figure out what it had been that ran him off. He spotted only one, but couldn't tell if it was really a track or just the way the gravel and dirt lay, like that "face" on Mars that could either be a face or a trick of the light depending on which direction the object was being viewed from. He sort of hoped this was the latter, because if something had been within ten feet of him last night and its foot was really that big, he didn't want to know about it.

He got back into Jessi's Range Rover and headed to another long day of freezing in the dairy cooler.

At least he'd remembered to bring his book.

On break a few hours later, David set himself a mere five-page goal until Mike Shelton sat down. He didn't mind Mike as much as he did Beth. Mike had never been one of his students and didn't feel the need to dig at him every chance he got. Mike was just a decent guy whose company David enjoyed.

"You're here today?" Mike said, sounding surprised.

"Of course," David said. "It's Sunday. I'm always here on Sunday."

"Yeah, I just didn't see your car outside. Thought you might have called in."

"I wish," David said, then told Mike about the accident.

"Holy shit!" Mike said at the end. "What was it?"

David shrugged and said, "No idea."

"Well, at least you made it out of there alive."

"Exactly."

"Did you see the paper this morning?"

David took a drink of his Coke, then shook his head.

Mike scanned the room, probably to see if there was a stray newspaper anywhere, but David didn't see any. Mike shrugged and said, "This chick over past Green Street, dude. They said someone broke in and trashed her house, tore her up pretty bad. Gutted her is what the paper said."

"It actually said she was gutted?"

"Okay, 'disemboweled', Professor. Same thing."

"That's crazy shit. What else did it say?"

"That was it," Mike said. He shrugged. "It was just last night, they probably didn't have much else *to* say."

"And who was it again?"

"Lisa Lumley?" Mike said. "You know her?"

"Sounds familiar," David said, trying to search his memory. "Not sure. I'd have to see her. Was there a picture in the paper?"

"Yeah, but I don't see one in here."

"Oh well. Break's about over anyway. That is fucked up, though."

"Yeah, so I guess a wrecked car don't look too bad, huh?"

"It's all perspective, dude."

David pocketed his book, grabbed his jacket off the back of his chair, and headed back to the dairy cooler.

He kept turning that name over in his head, knowing it held something he should remember. Lisa Lumley. Lisa Lumley. But whatever the truth of it was kept slipping from his grasp.

Finally, the day was over and it was time to head home.

David made the drive this time trying to keep his attention focused on the road and not imagine Ashley sitting next to him, engaging him in interesting conversation. That lasted about as long as it took him to make his way out of the parking lot. Soon, he imagined himself telling Ashley about the wreck and imagining how she would react. Surely, she would take the news better than Jessi had. Sure, it was a terrible thing, but it wasn't the end of the world. They would figure it out. He really couldn't understand her insistence on that level of attitude when things went wrong. It wasn't like he'd planned to wreck the car. Accidents happen. And no, he hadn't been texting!

Ashley wouldn't have even thought to accuse him of that, she would have just been happy it hadn't been worse.

She would have been happy he made it out alive. Ashley would have said, "Did you hear about Lisa Lumley? At least it was just a wrecked car, I can't imagine if that had been you that was attacked."

I almost was, he thought, and he knew that was the truth as soon as the thought formed. Whatever had been outside his window last night, if Parker hadn't come by in his truck when he did, David would have been in the newspaper this morning instead of Lisa Lumley.

Damn, I know that name, he thought.

Against every instinct in his body, David stopped at the spot again on the way home. It was dark now, and he definitely wasn't getting out of the car to inspect the sight, so why stop?

Because that name was connected to the spot somehow. If he could be here and try to figure out that connection, he might remember why he knew the name.

The field to the left stretched out to the woods that eventually became the Missouri River, across which, in Kansas, was the other half of Green Lake, more commonly called simply West, while the Missouri half was usually referred to as East, but both were, really, part of the same town. That is, if two thousand plus people could be considered a town. Surely that didn't qualify as a city, David thought.

To the right was another field, as this part of the state was lousy with them, and past that a small neighborhood. On Green Street, he thought, realizing that's where Mike said Lisa Lumley had been killed. He knew where Green Street was, of course, but he hadn't considered it was so close to the back road, just on the other side of the Christensen farm. And that's when he realized why he knew the name.

Lisa Lumley operated a daycare out of her home, on Green Street. She'd opened it over a decade ago. And before that, David was pretty sure she had babysat Alison and Victoria, when he was working third shift at a meat processing plant, going to school in the day, and sleeping in the evenings. Jessi hadn't been working, but was also in school, and Lisa watched the girls until Jessi came home in the afternoon.

And now she had taken something David couldn't help but feel had been meant for him. He didn't know that for sure, he didn't believe that whatever that animal had been it had sought him out specifically, but, again, if not for Parker, he was now one hundred percent certain he'd be on a slab instead of Lisa.

Christ, he thought. Morbid much?

He looked around again to make sure nothing was creeping up on him in Jessi's car. The area appeared to be empty. Despite the solitude, he shivered, then sped home.

• • • •

"AW, SHIT!" DAVID SAID the next morning while stepping into his pants.

"What?" Jessi asked from their bathroom.

"Do you have any cash on you? I forgot to go to the ATM yesterday, and I gave the girls' lunch money to Sandy for towing the car."

"I think I might have some," Jessi said. "What are you going to do about your car, by the way?"

He pulled on a T-shirt and was trying to decide what to wear over it.

"I don't know." He gave her Sandy's prognosis and asked, "What's your opinion?"

Jessi shrugged and said, "That's up to you. You know we need two cars, but can we afford to get that one fixed?"

"No more than we can afford a new one if we scrap it," David said, picking a light blue shirt and slipping into it.

"Well, we'll figure something out," she said. "I take it I'm taking you to work today?"

"Yeah," he said. "But I'll try to get a ride home from one of the other teachers." He found a grey tie and put it on.

"Then we'll have to leave early, so get ready."

"I just gotta get my shoes and my bag."

Jessi dropped David off at Green Lake High, then disappeared into the distance, on her way with Alison and Victoria to St. Vincent's. David had tried for a long time not to resent Jessi's position at the fancy school, while he was stuck in East, and for the most part he was able to stifle that feeling.

After all, Jessi had more education. David had his, too, but he'd also been working the whole time, trying to support his wife and daughters in addition to going to school. Jessi had been able to focus on school, and that dedication had won her the job. Good intentions counted for shit, Jessi was qualified. David liked to think he was, too, but that just went right back to good intentions.

Still, why should he be punished because he'd done the adult, responsible thing in those early years and gotten a job?

And that was why not resenting his wife—and to a lesser extent, his daughters—was sometimes easier said than done.

Stop your fucking whining, he thought. You've got a life a lot of people would kill for. Your wife loves you, even though she sometimes has a funny way of showing it. Your kids are happy and healthy, and lots of people can't find a job while you have two of them. Shut your trap and grow the fuck up.

• • • •

HALFWAY THROUGH THE day, he felt he may have hit upon why it was working in public school was so unsatisfying sometimes and it came when Jerome Hickman fell asleep in his class.

David woke him up by dropping one of the textbooks on the floor at Jerome's feet, shocking the kid, making him jump and yell, almost fall out of his seat, and causing the rest of the class to burst into laughter. Embarrassing Jerome Hickman wasn't the smartest move, it only made the boy want to listen even less, but David had a feeling no one else would be dozing off in his class any time in the near future.

He wondered if anyone ever fell asleep in Jessi's class. It's Sociology, he thought, of *course* they do. But somehow he doubted that was true.

The class dismissed and David had a free period, so he went into the teacher's lounge and fell onto one of the couches. He wished he was home, taking a nap. Really, he wished he was anywhere but here.

That's when he remembered he didn't have a way home yet. He climbed off the couch and looked at the time. He was going to ask Richard Moore, the boys' PE teacher and probably David's closest friend at the school. Richard's free period wasn't for another two hours, but it would only take a second to interrupt and ask.

David found the class about to start a game of basketball, so he waited until the ball was in play, then motioned Richard over. Richard gave his whistle to his TA, a young Mexican kid named Miho, then came over.

"I wrecked my car Saturday night. You mind if I get a ride home tonight?"

"Wrecked it?" Richard asked. "What happened?"

David told him the story, and Richard nodded and said, "Yeah, cool. I'll see you in the lounge after school."

"Cool, thanks," David said.

On the drive home that afternoon, Richard and his passenger traded stories about nightmare students, one of their favorite pastimes when they got together privately, and when they arrived, Richard pulled to the side of the road and let David out to walk up the driveway to his house on the hill.

"Thanks, man," David said, then closed the door and was headed up the drive before Richard had pulled away.

The wind was harsh tonight. He wondered if the carnival was still around, and if they were getting any business. He couldn't imagine being on those rides in this wind.

It was getting darker earlier and earlier every night. He couldn't believe the carnival was still in the area at all. If he were a traveler, he would have moved south weeks ago.

Lost in his musings, David stopped halfway up the hill to his house, suddenly stricken with the feeling he was being watched. He looked around, but the Reed property was bordered along the front by a ring of trees that blocked them from the back road. He didn't see anything on his property, and when he thought about it, he was pretty sure whatever was watching him wasn't doing it from so close.

He looked out past his yard, through the gap of his driveway. The only thing out there was the back road, the empty field across from that and, much further in the distance, the woods that led eventually to the river.

That's where it is, he thought. It's watching me from there. He thought of Lisa Lumley and whatever had been in the road Saturday night.

That's impossible, he told himself. That's got to be ... how many hundreds of yards away? Nothing could see him from there, not through this tiny break in the trees and definitely not in this light. It wasn't full night yet, but the sky was rotten with clouds and David was well hidden in the shadows of his trees.

Whatever's out there, he told himself, there's absolutely no way it can see me.

Yet, as he pulled the keys from his pocket, he couldn't help but feel that dread racing up his spine, telling him to get away, to get inside, shut and lock the door, and don't come out again.

Don't be a pussy, he tried to tell himself, but that feeling wouldn't let go. Finally, he gave into it and retreated inside before whatever was stalking him—and it wasn't just watching him, he felt that now; it was stalking him, like prey—could come out of the woods and show itself. Because whatever it was, he didn't want to see it. Not even a little bit.

• • • •

THAT NIGHT, DAVID HEARD something outside and his eyes opened to darkness.

What was that, he wondered. He tried to replay the sound in his head, trying to figure out what it was, but he'd been almost asleep and wasn't sure if it had been the beginning of a dream or reality.

He lay there a second and waited for it to come again.

There it was. But what was it? He sat up. The room was empty save himself and Jessi. He listened to the house. He was sure the girls were still asleep, as no sounds came from the hall. Whatever he'd heard had come from outside.

He got out of bed and went to the window. He tried to peer through parted blinds, but couldn't see anything, so he opened them instead.

Behind him, Jessi grumbled, "Close that and go back to sleep."

"Hang on," David said. "Heard something outside."

"There's nothing out there," she replied, but he was pretty sure she was already sleeping again before he could reply.

He closed the blinds and went downstairs.

In the kitchen, he got water from the fridge, guzzled it, then set the glass in the sink and looked out the back window.

There was something out there. Whatever had been watching him earlier, it had left the woods and was outside right now.

All he saw, though, were the woods at the edge of his property, two hundred yards back. The yard was empty. He detected faint traces of that curdled sock stench, but wasn't convinced that wasn't just a memory from the other night.

He went from room to room, looking out every window, knowing sooner or later he'd catch it, whatever it was. He thought briefly of calling the cops, but then played that scenario out in his head. They'd show up, lights flashing, and scare away whatever it was, and David would be left here looking like a pussy, or an idiot, probably both, with his wife and daughters looking at him in a way he didn't need.

But you heard it out there, he thought.

No, he'd heard something. They lived in the middle of nowhere, it could have been a raccoon in the attic.

No, it hadn't been inside the house.

Then again, he'd been half asleep—more than half—who knew what he heard or where it really was. There was every possibility it really had been a dream.

He took a final look through the front window, turning on the porch light, and was shocked when something reflected in the light. Something bright, something quick, something that was gone in less than the space of a blink.

What the fuck, he thought. That looked like—. He didn't let himself finish the thought. No, he decided, it wasn't what it looked like, because there's no way it could have been. It was a trick of the light, and his expectation.

It was a bat flying by, and the light from the porch caught it at just the right second. That's all.

He stood in the middle of the living room, staring at the window as if waiting for whatever that was to come back, but the house was silent save the ticking of the clock on the wall above the television. Trick of the light, he told himself again. That's all. Wrong place, wrong time. An accident of motion.

He made one final round of the house, checking every window, then making sure the doors were all locked, before going back up to bed.

It was a while before sleep found him again, and the whole time he kept seeing that vision in his head, the quick blur of motion, the color of it, the height. The eyes.

Whatever it was, it had been back in the trees. Maybe an owl?

It had to be. Because he knew with almost one hundred percent certainty that it had definitely been a set of eyes. But for them to be placed so high off the ground ... please let it have been an owl, he thought. An owl on a branch, and not some other animal, on the ground, with eyes that high. Because if that's the case, that would have to be one really big fucking animal.

Just an owl, he told himself over and over until he was pretty sure the sun was rising.

• • • •

TUESDAY BEGAN AS DAVID suspected it would.

"What are you going to do about your car?" Jessi had asked as David kissed the top of her head, then poured coffee into a Doctor Who travel mug.

"Not much I *can* do about it, is there? Unless you've got an extra thousand or so sitting around."

"Then you need to scrap it."

"Which leaves us right where we are now, with you driving me to work and picking me up."

"I thought you were at least getting rides home."

David grabbed a pack of Pop-Tarts from the pantry, knowing he wouldn't eat them, that the coffee would hold him over until lunch, but just in case.

"It's been one day. Rich never said he'd be my new taxi. Anyway, I've got a meeting with a parent afterward tonight."

"Why would you schedule a meeting after school when you don't have a car?"

"I didn't," David explained. "I scheduled it when I still had a car. This is the first time she can make it."

"Who is she?"

David shrugged and grabbed his wallet and keys from a table by the door.

"Mother of a student. He keeps skipping my class. Anyway, I don't know how long that'll take, but I'm not asking Rich to wait behind for me."

"So we have to come pick you up?"

"I could always walk," David offered.

"Fine," Jessi said. "What time should I be there?"

"Make it 5:00," David said. "Just to be safe. No idea how long the meeting'll take, but I've got plenty to grade until you get there if it's over quick."

"Fine," Jessi said again, then yelled up the stairs, "Let's go girls."

Alison and Victoria came down, loaded with backpacks and jackets and David joked, "Are ya ready kids?"

They both nodded and Victoria said, "Yep," and David mourned the growth of his little girls who, in better days, would have answered him with a hearty, "Aye aye, Captain!"

• • • •

HE SAT ON THE STEPS outside the front of the school later that evening, as the sun had already begun to set, wishing he'd brought a jacket tonight, and wondered where the hell his wife was.

Jessi was already half an hour late, and David had considered the possibility she had forgotten him. It wouldn't be the first time. He considered just walking home, but why would he when he had a cell phone in his pocket and could just call her and see where she was. But he knew how often she answered the phone when he called, especially if she was driving, and he'd decided he wasn't going to call until she was an hour late, at least. Out of spite, mostly, but also partly because he expected she was already on her way, and if he called her likely response would be something bitter. So he waited.

He looked around at the neighborhood outside the school, wondering what the people in the houses out there were up to. Somewhere someone was sitting comfortably in a chair, watching television, probably a "Friends" rerun or last week's "Chopped" on their DVR. Someone out there was in the kitchen, cooking dinner for a family. They were inside where it was bright and safe and warm and they felt loved by those around them.

Someone somewhere out there was reading a book. Someone out there was taking a nap. Someone out there was watching him.

He felt it as sure as anything. Their eyes crawled all over him and he suddenly couldn't breathe. He wanted to freeze like a statue and maybe they'd go away. He tried to see out there into the neighborhood and try to find them, peeking out a window, or from behind a corner. But all he saw were houses and more houses.

Then he had another thought. It wasn't someone watching him, it was some*thing*. It was the thing outside the car. It had found him in town and was stalking him.

He dug his phone from his pocket and dialed a number. A few rings and Mick Bewlay answered.

"What's up?" he said.

"What's up?" David replied. "What you doing?"

"Not much," Mick said. "Just out in the woods. Gotta check some stuff, you know?"

David knew. The Bewlays made their own liquor in stills they had hidden in the woods around the trailer where the brothers lived.

"What are you up to?"

"Just sitting here waiting," David said. "The wife is supposed to be on her way to pick me up from work. Wrecked my car a few nights back."

"What happened?" Mick asked.

David could hear the wind whipping past on Mick's end of the phone.

"Something jumped out at me from the side of the road," David said. "Scared the shit out of me, and I swerved and hit a pole."

"Holy shit. What was it? A bear?"

David shook his head, even though Mick couldn't possibly see it.

"No," he said. "I'm not sure, but I don't think it was a bear. It was big, though. It stuck around for a second outside my car and started growling. I don't think bears growl, do they?"

"No," Mick said.

"The really fucked up thing, though," David said, looking around the school to make sure no stray students heard the profanity, "is, ever since then I keep getting this feeling like whatever it was is still out there, watching me. Like just now. I'm just sitting here by myself, waiting for Jess, and I could swear I'm being watched. Isn't that fucked up?"

"Yeah," Mick said. "But it could be, though. I mean, not to freak you out or nothing, but it could be. Could have been a maniac or something that night, some loon escaped from an asylum somewhere."

"We don't have any asylums around here," David said.

"Well, I'm just saying. I'd be on the lookout is all."

"Thing is," David said, again looking around, this time to make sure no one heard him say what he was about to say.

"Thing is, and I'm not crazy, you know that. It wasn't a bear, I'm pretty sure. And it sounded like it might have been a wolf, but I mean this thing was monstrous. Easily three times bigger than any wolf I've ever seen. I didn't get a good look at it, though. I was afraid to make eye contact that night, but I've thought about it since then and there was definitely something … strange about it."

"Probably just a werewolf," Mick said, but he didn't laugh afterward.

"Well, of course," David said. "What else could it have been? And if it was, then there might be more of them on the loose because that same night, this woman who runs the daycare in town got mauled in her bed. So she's probably one too, now."

"Naw," Mick said. "That's not the legend. If you get bit or scratched by one, you become one. But getting killed by one just gets you dead. Hey, you heard that story about that preacher up in Angel Hill back about a hundred years ago or so? Him and his lady friend got slaughtered by something, then the preacher's kid went missing and was never seen again. Legend had it the boy was a werewolf and killed them when the preacher tried to marry the town slut and the kid didn't like it."

"Sounds like an awful lot of specific details for a hundred year old story," David said.

He looked around the neighborhood again, wishing that feeling of being watched would go away, but it lingered on. At least he had some company now to ease his anxiety.

"I'm just telling you what I heard," Mick said. "Hey, I gotta get off here, I'm at the place, gonna do the thing,"

"Cool," David said. "Gimme a call later on."

"Will do," Mick said, and they hung up.

David tried to close his blazer around himself against the chill, but it did no good.

Where the fuck was his wife?

If she wasn't here in ten minutes, he was calling her, and he wasn't going to be nice about it.

He felt those eyes on him still, from somewhere out there, and his mind's eye flashed on a brief image, a pair of yellow eyes peering out of the dark. In his head, he heard a loud, echoing howl, followed by the deep growl of a predator.

He hated to admit it to himself, but what Mick had said had, honestly, already occurred to him.

The carnival was in town, and that brought strangers. He was even almost sure the moon had been full that night. He could look it up online to double check, but he felt confident he was right.

And in that Wolfman movie with Lon Chaney Jr., he remembered the original werewolf that had bitten poor Larry Talbot had been a gypsy, and he had to admit a roving band of travelers would be pretty good cover for a curse like that, always in a new town, untraceable.

But not in this day and age, he thought. In today's world, anyone can find out anything anywhere at any time. There's no such thing anymore as the perfect cover. Most carnivals had websites, in fact, to let people know where they were going next.

Still, there was something about that idea that felt right to him. He decided he wanted to go by the carnival again and just watch them, see if he could pick out anyone who might be worth looking at again.

David was no detective, but he was a pretty smart guy, despite what his wife sometimes thought. Speaking of, he thought, look who's finally decided to show up.

He wanted to complain, to bitch her out for being so late. But he was just glad she was here finally, and it wasn't worth the argument, so he got in the car and kept his eyes out on the drive home, looking for something running alongside the car, hidden by shadow, but stalking them all the way.

He didn't see anything.

• • • •

THAT NIGHT, HE WAS woken again in darkness.

He lay in bed for a long time, just listening. He wanted to make sure something was out there before he panicked, but he couldn't deny this was the third night in a row he'd been woken up, so there had to be something. Didn't there?

David had always been the one to sleep wherever he was, if necessary. He could sleep in the car, on the couch, in a chair. On the nights Jessi complained she hadn't been able to sleep, David had been out like a light. But now he'd woken up every night this week, and he was sure it was noises outside the house that had done it.

Then a thought occurred.

What if it hadn't been a noise outside that woke him up. What if it was something inside the house?

And what if he heard it again?

He lay there quietly and waited. The anticipation was almost worse. He felt his heart pounding. He was going to hear it again and it was going to be on the stairs. No, it was going to be in the bedroom doorway. And it would be too late to do anything about it. Whatever was out there, whatever was after him, would attack before David had a chance to defend himself, or his wife. What if it didn't come after him? What if it went after one of the girls?

He got out of bed and went to the hall, scared, but determined to stop anything that might be out there before it could hurt his family.

The hall was empty, and dark, as he knew it would be.

You're making yourself paranoid, he thought. That's why you can't sleep.

Go back to bed. There's nothing out here.

He turned around and climbed back into bed, covered up and felt his wife's bare legs against his.

He lay awake, though, staring out the window. Something *was* out there. It hadn't made it inside the house. But it was out there. And who, or whatever it was, it wanted in. It wanted him.

WEDNESDAY

• • • •

THAT NIGHT AFTER WORK, David decided to take the family back to the carnival for one more night of fun before it left town. This was what he told them, anyway. Truth was, he wanted to do some reconnaissance and check out the suspects. He'd lived in Green Lake all his life, had known almost everyone in town that long, or at least been familiar enough to recognize the faces on the street. So who—or what—ever was stalking him every night, it had to be a stranger, he decided. And the only strangers in town were the carnies.

It's one of them, he told himself. He would take the wife and kids one more time and, while they had their fun, he'd keep an eye out for anyone who looked like they might be spending too much time watching him.

"I'm not going to the carnival again," Jessi told him.

"You might as well go while they're here," he said. "They hardly ever stop here."

"You need to save your money anyway," she said. "You need a car."

"One night at the carnival isn't going to change anything there. Come on, you'll have fun."

"No," she said. "I've got a headache anyway. If you want to take the girls, go ahead."

David didn't argue any further. He decided it would be easier to people watch without Jessi there anyway. So he gathered Victoria and Alison, both of whom seemed especially pleased for this mid-week break, and he headed out.

He paid for two bracelets, giving the girls unlimited access to whatever rides they wanted, as many times as they wanted them. On a Wednesday night, with the park nearly empty, the bracelets were a cheap ten bucks each. David passed on getting himself one, remembering how sick he'd gotten the last time. Anyway, he couldn't find his stalker if he was spinning and flipping upside down.

The girls hit the Ferris Wheel first, as it was just inside the gate. They said they were going to ride everything, making their way from one side of the carnival to the other and back around.

While they rode up, around, and down, over and over, David looked around, trying to seem casual. The shady characters abounded, though. It was going to be impossible to pick one of these guys out from the rest.

The air was a mix of that thick, sweet funnel cake smell with a light topping of cotton candy. He was amazed at how fast smells could bring back the past.

Man, he thought, the quality of life here hasn't changed much since I was a kid, has it?

It seemed everywhere he looked, he was greeted by the same sight. Permanently-tanned skin, faded tattoos, filthy hats. David didn't want to be the guy to stereotype, but it was kind of hard when the stereotype was staring him so blatantly in the face.

In fact, he thought, looking at them now, it wasn't so far beyond the realm of possibility to think one of these people just might be what Mick had said. A werewolf.

Of course the idea was as ridiculous as it sounded, but think about it logically. Most of the old time legends about werewolves didn't spring up because people back in the day honestly turned into wolves at the full moon. He knew many cases were actually cases of a mental disorder where the victim *believed* they were turning into a wolf and acted accordingly. And David wasn't naïve enough to think that, just because it was 2015 instead of 1015, that didn't automatically make certain mental disorders disappear.

There was every reason to believe one of these people here just might think he turned into a wolf during a full moon. David hadn't looked at the person, or whatever, outside his window. He'd only heard it. You get a big enough guy, make him just left of the middle mentally, you feel that hulking presence behind you, add in a growl, and who knew where the mind would take you.

So, okay, maybe he wasn't looking for an honest to God movie version werewolf, but that didn't make his search any less valid.

The girls had moved on to the Octopus, usually one of David's favorites to ride with them, when someone bumped into him from behind. He stumbled forward, almost hit the guard rail, and looked up.

One of the carnies, a short, thin guy in a Def Leppard concert T that had seen better days, with eyes that darted nervously about, motioned to him.

David looked around, saw there was no one else here, so he must be motioning to him. He looked over at the ride and saw the girls were safely encased and he could step away for a second. He followed the guy behind one of the columns supporting the overhead highway, thinking about the last time he'd been behind one of these, and his stomach suddenly flipped, threatening a repeat performance. He stamped it down.

Def Leppard looked around him and David wondered if someone were sneaking up on him, but then realized the guy was just scared.

"Do I know you?" David asked.

"You're not safe," the little man said. David could tell he didn't want to be here, that if he were caught, something bad might happen to him. He didn't know what, but it was obvious in the way the man kept looking around, over David's shoulder, over his own shoulder, off to the side. This guy was expecting trouble coming his way.

"Not safe from what?" David asked.

Who, he meant to say, but the "what" had come out first, because he knew that was probably closer to the truth. He could rationalize and assign diagnoses all he wanted, but it didn't take away the fear nor alleviate the danger.

"It watches you," the little man said.

"Who does? Who is watching me?" David asked.

"There's no man in there. It's all hunger. You're not safe."

Before David could ask anything else, the man took off running, into the field beyond the carnival, vanishing into the darkness. He wanted to chase after him, but he had kids here, and with that warning officially delivered, he sure as hell wasn't leaving them alone here. It was clear as day now, someone here wanted to hurt him.

He went to get the girls and get the hell out of here before something happened. He didn't want to prejudge anyone, but he had to consider the carnival was just like any other place of business; the people there stuck together.

Whoever here was the "monster", the others had obviously done a decent job of covering for him. Who was to say if it attacked him here in the open that the others wouldn't step in to make sure there were no witnesses? Or at least to turn a blind eye while David and his daughters were mauled like Lisa Lumley?

He ran back to the Octopus, which was somehow still running, but he didn't see his daughters on there. He kept watching, waiting for their car to spin around and reveal their ecstatic faces, but they simply weren't there anymore.

Where the hell were they? Someone had come and taken them. Def Leppard had been a distraction, he realized, to get him out of the way while they—"they" being "the carnival"—took his daughters away.

The panic he felt didn't settle in, it attacked him like a mountain lion and suddenly everything inside him wanted to scream. It felt like a trapdoor had opened inside his chest and his heart plunged a hundred stories down, crashing into a pile of broken glass and metal. His stomach filled with acid and his entire body was covered in a nervous sweat.

Where the fuck are they, he wondered, looking around the carnival grounds, hoping to see them being dragged off. It would be a heartbreaking sight, but at least he'd know where to go to follow them.

But there were no comical legs kicking wildly from behind a closing door, no black-caped evildoer absconding with his girls. They just weren't there.

He yelled for them, "Victoria! Ally! Victoria! Ally!"

He saw something moving out of the corner of his eye and he followed it.

It was Victoria, waving to him from atop the next ride over, the Viking Ship, swinging back and forth. They had simply moved on without him. The relief he felt in that moment was the most glorious thing to ever happen to him and he felt for one brief second like the world just might not be out to beat him down at every turn.

But Def Leppard's words came back and he knew that moment was gone again. It might not be life that was against him, but pretty much anyone telling you you're "not safe" was all the warning a mentally stable person would need.

As soon as the ride ended and the girls descended the ramp, he told them, "Okay, it's time to go. Sorry, girls, but I forgot I can't stay out too late, I've still got a lot of grading I have to get done before tomorrow."

"But can we just do one more ride?" Victoria asked. "I wanted to do the Chicago Loop again before we go!"

David wanted like nothing else to say yes and let them finish their fun, but he felt the eyes on him again. Whoever, whatever, was out to get him was somewhere in this crowd. He didn't want to accept it, he wanted to chalk up the entire past week to his own paranoia, but good Christ, he could almost feel the eyes drilling into his skin. They were here, somewhere, hiding from him but watching his every move.

And he couldn't take it.

"I'm sorry, Tori, I really can't. If I had remembered earlier, we probably wouldn't have even come, but I gotta get this stuff done."

"Man!" Victoria said.

So much for winning their favor by being the cool parent who takes them to the carnival in the middle of the week, he thought.

On the drive home, with the girls in the back of Jessi's Range Rover, both probably texting their friends to say how lame their dad was, he had a thought.

The carnival moves on at the end of the week. All he had to do was hold on a few more days and pretty soon they would be gone and, with them, whoever was stalking him.

He thought of maybe calling the police and letting them handle things, but then he realized he had absolutely not one shred of proof that anything, anyone, was really out there. All he had were a few nights of waking up in the middle of the night. All he had were a few instances of thinking he was being watched. That would never be enough to make the Green Lake PD search the grounds until they found the carny who thought he was a werewolf.

So he'd just have to be patient. Be careful, but don't panic and by this time next week all of this would be over.

• • • •

THAT NIGHT HE HEARD it again. He crept downstairs and went to the front window next to the door. He stood there, staring out into the darkness, trying to see those eyes. He didn't see anything, but he smelled it clear as fresh grass on a still summer day. That sour milk smell, like whatever it was had gone bad but hadn't yet realized it.

Everything was still again and he was beginning to wonder, once again, if he'd really heard anything at all.

The world was still, when he heard, "Dad?" from behind him.

David jumped and turned. It was only Victoria.

When he calmed down, he asked, "Hey, what are you doing up?'

"I heard something outside," she said. David froze, but didn't want to give himself away.

"It was nothing," he said. "Everything's okay, go back to bed. There's nothing out there."

Just then, something outside howled. Victoria's eyes went wide and David felt imaginary claws tracing a line up his spine.

"That's just animals in the woods," he told her. "It's okay. We live in the middle of nowhere."

"That doesn't make me feel better," she said.

"I promise," he lied. "Everything's okay. We've lived here how long, and they've never come out of the woods up to the house? Anyway, if they did, they'd be more scared of us."

"I doubt that," Victoria said.

"Go back to bed. I'll be here. I'll make sure the big bad wolf doesn't get you."

Victoria smiled at that, and went back upstairs. David wished he felt so sure about everything himself. He stood at the window for nearly an hour, but never heard another sound, nor saw anything outside. Finally, he double checked every lock in the house, then went back up to bed.

THURSDAY

• • • •

JESSI CALLED IN THE next morning, complaining of stomach cramps and a sore throat, so David had to leave extra early. He had to take Victoria and Ally to school in West, then drive all the way back to East to his own school.

"Bring a book," he told his daughters. "I'll get there as soon as I can afterward, but you're still going to have to wait."

He knew they hated waiting, but there wasn't much to be done about it this time.

On the way there, he decided to try to cheer them up. When they were younger, they always laughed when David turned on the radio and sang the wrong lyrics to songs. There was the popular "There's a bathroom on the right" to CCR's "Bad Moon Rising", or "Scuse me while I kiss this guy," to Hendrix's "Purple Haze". A Prince song, "Lemon Crush" contained the phrase "my animal-like persistence" and David always changed it to "my animal-like assistants", which never failed to crack them up.

He hit shuffle on his phone and got The Band's "Life is a Carnival", which David changed to "Life is a carnivore," but it only took a second before the realization of what he'd said hit him and he lost the urge to follow through with the rest of the song. And anyway, the girls weren't paying attention, so what was the point?

He dropped them off, gave them both a quick kiss, and said to have a good day before the girls were gone and he was alone again.

It was early and the sun was still struggling to find its way over the horizon, but it was technically day. So why did he feel so uneasy being out here all alone on the road, driving back across the river?

From the bridge, the small town of Green Lake appeared to be on its last legs. Very few lights burned, and the roads were deserted this early in the morning. He knew once he got into town, he'd see the traffic and the houses and the people all awake and moving about, but for that brief moment, David was struck by how isolated he felt just then.

He turned on the radio for some chatter and wound up with the tail end of REM's "Everybody Hurts" which made him think of Jessi. They used to listen to that song a lot together, and had seen the band live twice in the early years of their relationship. Back when they were young, dumb and in love, he thought. Before life came beating down their door and making demands.

Those were good times, he mused, even though they were always broke, had borrowed money from his parents more times than he cared to admit, and he'd spent so many nights eating spaghetti for dinner he'd eventually gotten sick of it. A big paycheck back then meant pizza and *two* movie rentals. That was a good night back then.

How things change, he thought.

The song ended and the DJ came on with the news, most of which David ignored, until the voice coming from the speakers said a man named Harvey Leonard from Rock Springs Road had been found dead on his front lawn in the middle of the night.

He'd come out, presumably, to deal with a noise on his property as Mr. Leonard was found with a rifle clutched in his hands. The report didn't say if he'd shot anything, but if he had, it either hadn't done any good or he hadn't done it soon enough.

Face down in the grass with his insides ripped out, gun at the ready, was no way to go, David thought.

Two in a week, he thought.

Don't let me be the third, he thought.

For a change, he was glad to get to work, to be standing in front of his students, in a room full of warm bodies, verifying that, no matter how things seemed sometimes, he really wasn't alone in the world.

Unfortunately, that feeling didn't negate the past week, so on lunch he went outside and called the Bewlays to see if they had any insight.

Mick answered again and David asked, "Is Donny ever home anymore?"

"Not often," Mick said. "He's out checking the stills."

"Why do you guys hide those things out in the middle of nowhere? I never got that. You do know it's legal to produce your own liquor in this state. I mean, not on a massive scale, but for how little you two make, for your own use, you don't have to hide them."

"Yeah," Mick said, "but what's the fun in that?"

"You guys are weirdos," David said.

"And you're the one calling," Mick said. "What's up?"

"Oh, nothing big," David said. "I was just wondering is all."

"Wondering what?"

"You remember what I was telling you the other day? About wrecking my car, then feeling like something was following me?"

"Uh huh," Mick said and David wondered if he was even listening or if he was too busy flipping through a skin mag, which wouldn't have surprised him.

"Well, I got to thinking," David said, trying to figure out how to ease into the conversation without sounding like the superstitious backwoods hick he knew he was going to sound like anyway. "Do you guys know of anything that might be in the woods around here? Animals or something? I assume you guys get stuff roaming past your place all the time at night, but I keep hearing stuff outside my house now and I'm afraid something is going to come right up to the house. Last thing I need is a wolf scratching at my back door at three in the morning."

"Still got that werewolf problem, huh?" Mick asked. David heard the flipping of a page in the background and Mick sounded bored.

"Yeah, that's probably still it," David said. "Seriously, should I be worried?"

"About werewolves?"

"About something coming out of the woods and trying to get in my house."

"I don't see why," Mick said. "I mean, there are reports of wolves trying to get inside, but I don't know that any ever have. No opposable thumbs, right? Can't turn the knob."

"But they have tried to get inside before?"

"Well, not recently, that I know of, and not around here. I'm talking I read about something in one of the Dakotas, over a hundred years ago. Houses were a little less secure back then, you know?"

"Okay," David said, trying to worm his way into the real conversation now. "But, have you guys heard anything out there by where you live? I'm not even saying it is a wolf I hear; I don't know what it is. But I know there's something out there. And with that Lumley girl getting killed, and now this other guy. Something obviously tried, and made it into their houses."

There was silence on the line for a second, then Mick said, "Well, yeah, I didn't think about that."

"Okay, then, so I should be worried?"

"Nah," Mick said. "I wouldn't be."

David had walked three laps of the playground by now and he wondered how much time he had left. He still hadn't eaten anything.

"Have you heard anything about that girl?" he asked. "Did they ever figure out what did it, and how it got into her house?"

"Don't know," Mick said. "I haven't been to town this week."

"Cool. Let me know if you do hear. I'm curious, and she wasn't too far from my house. I got daughters I gotta protect."

"My money's on an ex-boyfriend," Mick said. "I heard she used to be called Peanut Butter Legs back in the day."

"Do what?" David asked.

"She spread for bread, man. That's what I heard anyway. Girl like that, who knows who she had in her past. Lotta crazies around here."

"That's what worries me. Hey, if you think of anything else, call me."

"I will," Mick said.

"And tell Donny it won't kill him to be at home once in a while."

"No shit. Half the time I feel like I'm out here all by myself."

"I don't see how you do it. I'd be too freaked out to sleep out there in the middle of nowhere like that."

"You get used to it."

"Oh," David said. "Before I forget, *have* you heard any stories around here?"

"Like what kind?"

David shrugged, even though Mick couldn't see it, and said, "I don't know. Legends or whatever."

"No stories of werewolves during the full moon, no," Mick said, and David could tell he wanted to laugh.

"Just checking," David said.

"I wouldn't lose any sleep over it," Mick said. "Just forget it. Whatever it is, if there even is anything, and it's not just your overstressed imagination, it's not going to try to pick your locks. It might rummage through your trash. Hell, that's probably it, you got raccoons. But that'd be about the worst of it, I'd say. Just relax."

"Cool," David said. "Thanks. But let me know if you find out what happened to those people."

"I will."

They hung up and David went inside, feeling a little better after Mick's assurances, and ate his lunch.

· · · ·

DAVID RUSHED THROUGH town and across the river to Green Lake West to pick up his daughters after school and get them home, fed, and to their respective Thursday night activities.

Jessi had given them a list several years earlier and said, "Pick one." She insisted the girls participate in an extracurricular activity to keep them from becoming one of those teens who sit in their room all night and never socialize with other kids their age. Alison had picked swimming while Victoria went a little more adventurous and chose archery.

Up until this past weekend, they'd taken turns, since both took place at the same time. David would take Victoria to archery while Jessi took Alison to swimming, and the next week they swapped. But with only one car now, tonight was going to be a little more hectic.

They ate a quick frozen pizza, then he packed them back into Jessi's car—she was still in bed, coughing and sweating—and rushed to drop off first Victoria, then Ally.

He had a couple of hours to kill then, so he sat in the waiting area of the pool and graded papers.

That was the plan, anyway. But his mind kept drifting.

He just kept thinking about that carnie telling him he was in danger. David didn't want to believe it, of course. Who would? But that doesn't just happen. People don't just confront you and say you're in danger. Unless there's some reason for it.

And while he wouldn't admit it out in the open to anyone but himself, he knew there was some part of him that wasn't totally closing the door on the werewolf angle. Yes, they were myths, they were monsters and there was no such thing as monsters. But the legend came from somewhere. And who among us, he thought as he sat there under the lights with the sound of splashing and starting whistles in the next room, hadn't taken the trash out late one summer night only to think of that scene in *An American Werewolf in London* where the two party-goers were attacked and killed on their way down the sidewalk.

That was part of the movie's brilliance, that such an impossible, terrible thing could happen in even the most populated places. The clash of ancient myth and the modern world. And other than telling himself over and over there was "no such thing", David couldn't think of one good reason why it couldn't be possible here, too, in Green Lake.

Besides, he wasn't imagining the noises he heard in the night. He sure as hell hadn't imagined the hulking shape snarling outside his car that night. Whether werewolf or just a run of the mill madman, this past week had been haunted by something he wasn't prepared to face.

And it had all started when the carnival came to town. The carnie had told him he was in danger. He knew something.

David looked at the time and saw he still had an hour before either girl would be done.

He packed up the papers he had stopped grading a while ago and snuck out the door. The carnival was only a few minutes away and he saw it was packed pretty tight for a Thursday night. That was going to make this more difficult, if he could even remember what the guy looked like.

He got out and walked past the ticket booth without stopping. Admission was free, after all, and he wasn't riding anything tonight.

He was surprised at how many people were there. He had always thought of Green Lake as being a one stoplight town, but he knew it was bigger than that. The population was almost five thousand, after all, and he wouldn't have been surprised if someone told him they were all at the carnival that night.

They must be out for one last hurrah before the carnival moved on.

He breezed past the rides, looking at the workers and trying to spot the one from last night. It wasn't as easy as he'd hoped it might be, though; they really did all sort of look alike. He knew how bad that sounded, but it was the truth.

There hadn't been anything memorable about the guy, and he'd been a little too shocked to really bother memorizing any of the details.

He decided to scout out the rides they had hit that night, since the man had come to him. He headed for the Octopus, the ride the girls had been on at the time. He walked around the ride's perimeter, watching everyone and trying to see if any of the workers recognized him.

When none did, that he could tell, he went back one ride, with the same effect. Then he moved on to the Chicago Loop, which had been next in line that night. Still, none of the workers gave him a hint of recognition. He turned around, toward the rides on the opposite side of the park, still trying to see through the crowd.

That's when he felt the eyes on him. David scanned the faces, knowing someone out there was watching him. Anonymous forms brushed past him, crowds of colors and shapes blurring through his field of vision, confusing his eyes.

The sounds of the park rang in his ears, music blasting from too many speakers.

Then he spotted him. The man stood by the gate, watching him with an intensity David could feel from his spot halfway down the park. He wore the same Def Leppard T-shirt.

He locked eyes with the man and David held him in his gaze as he walked with a purpose through the crowd, stalking toward the man as David himself had been stalked. The man remained frozen, a look of fear on his face as David stopped in front of him.

"What the hell did you mean last night," he asked. "You said I was in danger."

The man was obviously terrified to even be near him.

"Were you trying to threaten me?" David asked.

"No," the man muttered.

"Then what the fuck, man?"

"You're not safe," the carnie said, simply repeating his previous warning.

"Yeah, you said that already, and I want to know what the hell that means."

As before, the carnie didn't answer.

"Who is after me?" David yelled at him.

The carnie looked past David's shoulder and David thought Here we go, the manager's coming over to break it up and kick me out.

He glanced backward to make sure he wasn't taken by surprise when the big, muscle-bound hands grabbed him and threw him out, but instead he didn't see anything but the same anonymous swirls of color and form that was the people of Green Lake on a Thursday night. When David turned back, Def Leppard was gone.

David looked backward again, wondering now what the hell the carnie had been looking at. He wondered if the werewolf was in the crowd. Not in wolf form, obviously, but whoever it was here that had that hidden inside him, whichever of these wanderers used the carnival as the perfect cover to move around and not be discovered.

He looked for anyone who might be looking in his direction, or walking this way, but the chaos of the crowd was just too much to untangle and he suddenly felt very claustrophobic, like the people were about to press in on him and smother him.

He wanted to run back to the car, back to the swim center, back to the life he had a week ago.

Something slapped him on the shoulder and David uttered a quick yelp of panic before whirling to find it was only Mick Bewlay.

"What the fuck, man?" he said. "Don't do that!"

"Sorry," Mick said, trying not to crack up with laughter. "I didn't mean to scare you, I thought you saw me a second ago. You looked right at me."

"Did I? Man, I didn't even see you. You scared the shit out of me, though."

"Sorry about that. What are you doing out here? You bring the family?"

David looked around, as if he needed confirmation before answering.

"No," he said. "The girls are at their things, their after school stuff. Wife's home sick."

"So you just came out here to ride the Ferris Wheel all by yourself?"

David was still scanning the crowd while trying to look like he wasn't scanning the crowd.

"No," he said again. "I mean, we brought the girls last Friday. I was just here looking for something."

"What are you looking for? I'll help."

"That's okay," David said. "I mean, I was looking for one of the workers. I had to ask him about something, but he bailed on me and now I can't find him again."

"Just ask one of the others," Mick suggested.

David shook his head, feeling kind of stupid now that there was another familiar face in front of him, talking to him like he was a normal human being.

"Shit," he said, remembering he had a life outside these grounds. "What time is it? I gotta get the girls."

Mick looked at his watch and rattled off the time, but David didn't even hear him. He did one last quick scan of the grounds, but Def Leppard was nowhere in sight.

"Hey, before I go," he said, "you guys are real good at all that pioneer, make it yourself stuff, right?"

"Of course. Only way to live. Hunt your own food, building your own house, make your own way in the world."

"Cool," David said. "Do, uh, you think one of you guys could make something for me?"

Mick shrugged. "I could give it a try."

"Can you make me a silver bullet?"

Holy crap, he thought, I can't believe I said it out loud. And after a second ago when I was starting to feel normal again. But it's out there now. All I can do is see what he does with it.

"And why, again, do you need one of those?" Mick asked, scratching the scruff of matted, uncombed and uncut brown hair on top of his thick head. "You hunting werewolf?" He chuckled after that.

David laughed along with him and tried not to look guilty.

"No, I'm thinking ahead," he improvised. "Halloween's coming up, I was gonna be the Lone Ranger. Just trying for a little authenticity."

"I see," Mick said, obviously not believing David's explanation. His doubt shone clear on his face. He scratched at his cheek and said, "Well, see the problem with silver is, it melts at a higher temperature than, say, lead, so you'd need a furnace. We have the woodstove in the trailer, but I can't promise that would work, either. Also, silver shrinks a lot more than lead, so you use a standard case and the slug won't fit. Just buy some plastic silver bullets at the Dollar Store."

"Yeah, but that wouldn't be the same, now would it?" David reasoned.

"Anyway," Mick continued, "silver bullets don't really stop werewolves. That was added later, probably invented with the Beast of Gevaudan story."

"Show off," David said.

"Not to burst your bubble, of course. Trust me, being the smart one in the room isn't all it's cracked up to be," Mick said, grinning.

"I wouldn't know," David said. "Well, I'll think of something. I better get the girls. I'll talk to you later."

• • • •

HE FOUND HIMSELF WORRYING on the drive back. With Mick's latest bit of info, now what was he supposed to do? He hadn't realized how much of his hopes had been pinned on the Bewlays helping him out, but now that he saw that wasn't going to happen, he felt somewhat lost.

He picked up the girls one at a time, then drove home and they had another quick bite while Jessi was still in bed. David wondered what she had and how long it would be before he and the girls caught it.

While the girls finished their homework, David set up camp in the kitchen with his laptop and did a little research. He tried to remember what Mick had said about silver bullets, but the name of the story escaped him. Finally, through a few rabbit hole searches, he stumbled upon it.

The Beast of Gevaudan, he read, dated back to France in the 1760s where a large wolf-like creature was held responsible for at least sixty deaths. Eyewitness accounts varied as to the beast's true form with many different variations on the coloring alone—some speculated this may be proof there was more than one animal at work—but most of the stories agreed on one thing, at least. The Beast of Gevaudan could not be killed by bullets until one man shot it with a silver bullet.

David wondered how, if someone shot and killed the beast, there could be any doubt as to what it looked like. Surely Jean Chasetl, the man credited with "killing" it got a good look. Then again, this was the internet, he reminded himself, and that meant all bets were off as to whether the Beast of Gevaudan was even a real thing.

Still, it did make him wonder about the idea of the silver bullet. He wondered what was so special about them, why silver was said to be the thing to stop a werewolf, and why a lead bullet wouldn't be just as effective. Getting shot is getting shot, right?

But if we're talking werewolves, he thought, why rule out the possibility of silver having some kind of magical effect? I mean, sure, the idea of the magic bullet is a ridiculous notion in a real world scenario, but so is the idea of a man who turns into a wolf, but isn't that exactly the thing you're considering?

He wasn't sure how far he wanted to take that line of reasoning. He kept trying to tell himself he lived in the real, waking world of physics and logic, but in the middle of the night, when he felt that presence outside his house, when the darkness and the shadows concealed so much from him and the sounds he heard weren't the normal sounds he was used to when the lights were on...it made a guy wonder. The world seemed a much safer place in the daytime.

Finally it was bed time and he kissed the girls goodnight. Before he left Victoria's room, his hand reaching for the light switch, she asked, "Leave it on?"

"It's late," he said. "Time for bed."

"I know," she said. "I just don't want the light out yet. I'll get it in a minute."

He looked at her face and asked, "What's wrong, Tori?"

"Nothing," she shrugged. "I just don't want to be scared."

"There's nothing scary in here," David said.

"Not in here."

He suddenly knew what she was talking about. David came into the room and closed the door so Jessi couldn't hear if she got up.

"Tori, there's nothing out there. Nothing that hasn't always been there the whole time. There are lots of animals in the country, but we're perfectly safe. Here, would it make you feel better to sleep with the bow next to your bed?"

Victoria shrugged, but he knew she wanted to nod. He handed her the bow.

"If whatever we heard howling the other night comes back, I'll call animal control, okay?"

She nodded then.

"Just make sure, if you hear something, it's not your sister or mother in the hallway going to the bathroom. We do not shoot family, got it?"

Victoria laughed and said, "I won't."

He kissed her again and closed the door, leaving the light on for her.

He went to bed, hoping he didn't hear it again in the night, knowing he would.

• • • •

SO WHEN HE WOKE UP a few hours later, he was disappointed but not surprised.

He tried to comfort himself with the knowledge that, whatever it was, hadn't tried to get in yet, but that did little for him.

He wanted to lie there until the sounds went away, but that only left him feeling like a grade A pussy. You've got a family to protect, he told himself. That was all the motivation he needed. As much as he didn't want to face whatever reality might be out there, he wanted even less for his daughters to face it.

He got out of bed and went into the hall. He listened to the house. He didn't hear anything downstairs, but there was definitely something outside. He felt it in the chills running up his back.

He opened Ally's door, but she was out. He went to Victoria's room, stopped outside the door and heard something inside. He opened the door.

Victoria sat curled up on the bed, bow in hand, arrow nocked and ready.

"Are you gonna call?" she asked, whispering.

"It's just a wild animal," David said. "You're all right. I'll take care of it."

He thought about Lisa Lumley and Harvey Leonard and wasn't so sure.

He closed her door and went downstairs, out to the garage. Something shifted in the moonlight coming in from outside and he ducked down, into the shadows, hoping it wouldn't spot him.

It took way too long to find what he was looking for in the dark, but there wasn't a chance he was turning on the light. He knew roughly where it was, though, and he finally pulled it out. He tested the weight of the aluminum bat in his hands and thought, Well, it's not silver, but it's the best I've got.

Then he went into the dining room and opened one of the glass doors in the front of the hutch. The Reeds owned what David had been led to believe at the time was a set of sterling silver flatware from his wedding. He'd never had reason to doubt its authenticity before, but fishing out a fork from the unopened box at two in the morning with something stalking him outside, he just prayed there would be silver if he needed it.

He looked outside. The yard was, as usual, empty, so far as he could tell. Whatever was out there was good at staying out of sight. But he didn't doubt for a second there was something out there.

He stood at the window so long, peering through the blind, that he felt exhaustion weighing him down and David began to feel dizzy. He sat on the couch to keep from falling, all the while telling himself over and over, There's no such thing as werewolves, it's a wild animal from the woods.

Then why aren't you calling animal control like you told Victoria you would? The answer was simple. Because if it really was just something from the woods, something that, in all their time in this house, had never bothered to come closer before, then animal control could easily deal with it. But if it wasn't something from the woods, if it was something that spent its days working in a filthy carnival and its night terrorizing David and his family...he didn't want to be responsible if it attacked anyone who might show up here.

I just need to make it two more days, he told himself. The carnival will be gone by then.

But, he thought, in those last few moments before sleep overtook him again, what if whatever's out there knows its time is limited and is going to make sure it strikes before the carnival has moved on and it loses its chance?

Then I have to be ready, he thought, and spent the night sitting up on the couch, bat clutched in his lap, dreaming of hunting and killing a ferocious beast with nothing but a handful of wedding forks.

....

HE SLEPT LATER THAN he meant to, woke on the couch with a crick in his neck and his knees ached when he stood. Then his feet began to wake up and he had to sit back down until that process was over. He looked around the house. He heard activity upstairs, his daughters in their rooms. Jessi must still be in bed. He hoped they didn't catch what she had, but knew that wasn't how it worked and pretty soon he and the girls would be laid up in bed, forcing Jessi to take care of all of them. That wasn't going to be fun. Maybe he'd just overdose on orange juice and try to knock the bug out before it took hold.

He finally got up and started moving, took a shower, got himself dressed, then, with the water still running in the bathroom to hide the noise, he called in to work, taking the day off from school.

He dressed for work, gave his wife a peck on the forehead, which was burning up, grabbed a package from the dining room hutch, snuck out the door before anyone came down and saw what he had, stashed it in the back of the Range Rover, then called the girls down for school.

After dropping them off, he drove into the business district, if it could be called that in such a small town. For Green Lake, this meant two blocks where most of the older stores were located. There were two clothing stores, a jeweler, a pawn shop, a bank, three gas stations, one insurance office, two payday loan stores, a Dollar General, and an antique shop. He pulled into the parking lot of this last one and saw they were open.

David carried the silver set inside and when the short thin man behind the register saw him and asked, "Can I help you today?" David set the silverware on the counter and asked, "Can you tell me if these are silver, or just silver-plated?"

"I sure can," the thin man said.

He took the box from David and slid out one of the spoons. He turned it over, looking for something, David didn't know what, then set it down on the counter.

"One second," he said, and disappeared into the back. He returned thirty seconds later with what looked like a file in one hand and a small clear plastic bottle in the other.

"What we do," he said, "is look for markings on the item that say 'Sterling' or an abbreviation of it, but I don't see any on these. So what I'm going to do is file a small groove in it to get underneath." He set the file and bottle on the counter, then tipped the bottle toward David. "This is nitric acid. Silver reacts to this differently than other metals. If I apply a little of this to the area around the groove and it turns a creLisa white color, we've got silver. If it's not silver, we'll get green bubbles. If it's just silver-plated, we'll get creLisa white around the outside and a green mark in the center. Ready?"

David nodded, fascinated and hopeful.

The man turned the spoon over and filed a small groove in the underside of the handle.

"You'll want to step back a little," he said, picking up the bottle of acid. David did as he suggested.

He put the spoon on a folded white cloth, took the cap off the bottle, and squirted some of it onto the handle around the file mark. David watched it spill off and hit the cloth. What he didn't see was green bubbles. He smiled inside.

"Good to go," the man said. "Do you want me to test another one?"

David shook his head. Then he asked, "So is the whole thing silver?"

"Not on these," the thin man said. He held up one of the knives. "The handles on these, if they're the same as this spoon, are going to be silver, but," he held the knife closer for David to see. "The blades on these are stainless steel, see?"

David nodded, even though he didn't see whatever the man was expecting him to see.

"Cool, but the handles are silver?"

The man nodded, then asked, "Were you hoping to sell these today?"

David shook his head.

"No, my wife would kill me. They were a wedding gift. I just wanted to see how cheap her parents were."

The man nodded and gave David a knowing smile.

"Well if you change your mind, we do buy silver, and we could probably give you a pretty good deal for these. So just keep it in mind."

"I will," David said, sliding the pieces the man had taken out back into the box. "Thanks a lot."

He walked out, feeling a little bit of hope for the first time in days.

Back in the car, he set the box aside and pulled out his phone. He called Mick Bewlay, who answered...eventually.

"What's up?" Mick asked through a sleepy haze.

"You're still sleeping?" David asked. "Don't you got fields to hoe or something?"

"Hardy har. What time is it?"

"Almost eight thirty," David said. "Time to get up."

"Gimme a second."

He heard the phone being set down. There was a groan, probably Mick getting up and stretching the sleep out of his bones. A loud yawn. A crinkle of plastic, Mick getting a cigarette from a pack next to his bed. The faint flick of a lighter. Finally, Mick came back.

"Okay, what's up?"

"Can you guys do me a favor?" David asked.

"We can try," Mick said.

"Okay, don't judge me, but do you think you can melt down my silver wedding set?"

"I already told you, get the plastic bullets, they're just as good."

"Not for that," David said. He wasn't sure how much to tell Mick. He knew the Bewlays wouldn't believe him, but they'd been friends long enough they should be able to ask favors of each other with few questions asked. "I need a knife."

"A what?"

"A knife. I know, you said you'd need a furnace for silver, but you've got the woodstove and that's pretty much a furnace, isn't it?"

"No," Mick said. "It's not."

"No," David agreed. "But the melting point of silver is nine hundred sixty one degrees. A good wood fire can get up to eleven hundred degrees."

"Now who's showing off?" Mick said.

"The internet is a wonderful tool. So, can you do it?"

"You want what, again?"

"A knife," David said.

"And where do I get this silver?"

"I've got it right here. Wedding present."

"Aw, man, Jessi's gonna kill you."

"I'll worry about that later."

"So what do you want me to do?"

"I'm gonna bring it to you, you're gonna melt it down and make me a knife. A long, sharp hunting knife. I mean, the handle doesn't need to be silver, just the blade. But you have to watch out because the blades on these knives I've got are only stainless steel—just the handles are silver. But it's a pretty big set, so you shouldn't have any problem at least making the blade."

"What the hell do you need a silver knife for?"

David thought of the sight of Victoria sitting up in bed, terrified, bow and arrow ready to release if something came into her room.

"Just a precaution," he said. "So can you?"

He could hear Mick's shrug through the phone.

"I guess," Mick said. "I mean, I'll try anyway. No promises. I'm not a damn cutler, dude."

"You're everything else," David said. "And I'd trust you guys to do it over doing it myself any day."

"Yeah well, some of us got skills, and some of us need a wife to take care of us."

"And some of us get poon on the regular."

"I highly doubt that."

"Yeah well," David said, then offered his own silent shrug.

"I guess you can bring it over tomorrow and I can try to get started?"

"Can I bring it today?" David asked.

"Not gonna be here most of today," Mick said. "Gotta take off in a bit."

"How about if I drop it off today, and you guys'll have it when you get home tonight?"

"That might work," Mick said. "I think if we get started later tonight at least, then you could pick it up tomorrow?"

"That's quick. Awesome, perfect."

"No promises, though. I'm not even sure it's gonna work. I don't know what you think we do out here all day, but making weapons ain't it."

"Shit," David said. "You two put your minds to it, I don't think there's anything in the world you couldn't do."

"You're too kind," Mick said. "You're a pain in my ass, but you're too kind."

"What are friends for?"

"I'm still trying to figure that one out."

"Whatever, fucker. I'll bring em by. Thanks, too. I'll pay you for the labor."

"Yeah, I'll sweat over a hot oven for you for hours on end, you'll pay me back with a cold beer."

"Nah," David said. "I'd buy at least a six pack."

Before heading to the Bewlays' trailer, he swung by where the carnival was set up. He parked down the street and watched. It was still early, too early for operating, but the workers were up and readying for the day. He wondered which one of them it was who was after him.

"I'm gonna be ready for you," he muttered to whichever one it was. "You're time's almost up."

He really wished Mick and Donnie could get the knife forged today; he'd like to have it tonight. He could feel time running out. Pretty soon, tonight, maybe, if he was lucky, tomorrow, it was going to stop toying with him. No later than Monday, he thought, it was going to attack.

As he watched the carnies hustle about in the lot under the highway, he wondered if whoever was stalking him could sense him there. He wondered if a chill were running up a grimy back somewhere out there. Did someone feel his eyes on them?

He hoped they did, and he hoped it worried them.

He also hoped his baseball bat would be up to the task if tonight turned out to be the night. Maybe if he stopped wasting time here and got the silver to Mick and Donnie early enough, they could actually get it done tonight. He pulled away and drove to the woods where the Bewlays lived.

It was always hard to tell, just from looking, if anyone was home when you got to the Bewlay property. The place wasn't exactly run down, it was just ... not well-maintained. The Bewlays always claimed that was on purpose. Look like you've got nothing and people leave you alone.

"You guys live in the middle of nowhere," David said. "No one's coming all the way out here to burgle your house."

"Never underestimate the stupidity of the human race," Donnie had replied.

David had only shrugged at that. Now, he only had his knowledge of the two to tell him they weren't home: Mick's truck was gone.

David got out and approached the trailer. He shook his head at the look of it. The siding had at one time been white, but was now more grey and brown. He doubted the windows had ever been cleaned.

Sometimes he couldn't believe the state the Bewlays lived in. David, Mick and Donnie had practically grown up together in Green Lake. They'd met in middle school and immediately hit it off when they kept seeing each other in the school library after school. David was reading science fiction novels by the handful while the Bewlays were making their way through the horror section. The Bewlays finally struck up a conversation one day and they all became fast friends.

When he thought of how they'd been back then compared to how they were now, he sometimes had trouble rectifying they were the same pair of brothers he'd spent his senior year cruising through their small town with when he got his license. Then he would have a conversation with one of them and it would all come back. They were the Bewlay Brothers, and they were his best friends.

He had tried to pinpoint the moment their interests had begun to veer away from David's, and every time he thought about it it all came back to their father being arrested for tax evasion. It hadn't felt like a very big deal at the time, he was only going away for a year. The social stigma hadn't bothered the Bewlays, they had already formed their opinions of people in general and it wasn't one that worried what others thought of them. The problem was their father had died in prison when a fight broke out and he'd somehow been caught in the middle of it.

It didn't take long for Mick and Donnie to start retreating even further from society. After graduation, David had gone to college and when he came back he found the Bewlays had bought their trailer in the woods and were working toward becoming completely self-sufficient. They grew or hunted as much of their own food as they could. Their mother had died while David was away at school, and the boys sold the family home. With some of that money, they installed solar panels on top of their trailer, cutting themselves off from the Green Lake grid. They heated the place with their woodstove. The only thing they needed from the city was water. They had a single cell phone between them, pre-paid, which they swapped out regularly.

David knew the Bewlays to be the smartest two people he'd ever met, both of them mostly self-educated through constant reading and keeping themselves informed. The only flaw he could find in them, he thought, was their incessant hatred and mistrust of the government. Not that he didn't understand, after what had happened to their father, but if Mr. Bewlay had paid his taxes like everyone else, he'd never have wound dead in jail. David never said this out loud to them—he wasn't stupid and he valued their friendship—but it was a truth he carried inside all the time.

But they kept to themselves and they weren't hurting anyone out here away from everyone else, so what difference did it make?

He set the box of silverware on the porch, then put a couple of pieces of firewood over it, mostly to keep anyone who *might* happen by, as unlikely as that was, from seeing it right away and taking off with it.

He looked out into the small field beside their property, admiring the work they'd done out here. He knew from an early age that farming wasn't his thing, and he joked with them about toiling in the fields, but they'd set up a pretty good little plot out here, he had to admit, and he envied it.

He thought he heard something behind him. He turned and listened. It sounded like it came from inside, but he was pretty sure the guys weren't here.

He knocked on the door and waited, but no one came, nor did he hear it again. He put his ear to the door and knocked again.

"Dude," he called, "you in there? You ok?"

He tried to look in the window, but it had been covered by a sheet, as had all the windows in the Bewlay trailer. He tried knocking and listening one more time, but whatever he'd heard was silent now. If he'd heard anything at all. He knew lately he'd been becoming more and more paranoid and on edge. Something was coming to a boil, he felt, and he just hoped he could survive when it blew, whatever it was.

He looked at the silverware he'd left for Mick and Donnie and hoped that, when it did happen, whatever "it" turned out to be, he could be ready.

He went back to the carnival for another glimpse, one more attempt at spotting the one responsible for all his troubles lately. Then he went home and told Jessi he'd left work early, that he felt like he was getting whatever she had.

• • • •

HE WOKE UP THAT NIGHT, knowing this was it. He heard it, clear as anything, and the panic that rushed through him was a hopeless feeling, swallowing him whole. It had come to the house and he heard it down there, scratching at a window, taunting him.

David had only the briefest moment of paralysis where he wanted to hide up here and wait for it to go away, but he banished that thought right away. He only had his aluminum bat, but if that was the best he could do, it would have to be enough. He couldn't let this thing get to his family.

I should have insisted, he thought. I should have told them I need it today. I should have offered to pay them, whatever they asked for. The Bewlays weren't above bribing; he knew that from experience.

He had plenty of regular knives in the kitchen, but what could they do against what David was facing?

He had his bat clutched tight in his hands, and he crept out to the hall, ears tuned to everything around him. He knew if he heard it scratching, Victoria probably did, too. He imagined her in her room, curled up again with her bow ready. He would just have to do whatever it took to make sure nothing got close enough to her to make using it necessary.

Besides, what kind of man would he be to rely on his kid to protect him?

God, I should have made sure they did it today, he thought.

He made his way down the stairs, listening and waiting for that crash of glass as it broke in to kill him.

It scratched again, tapped at the glass, beckoning him, mocking him.

He tried to take a breath, but found his chest had tightened. His jaw quivered in fear, but he had made up his mind to face whatever was waiting for him down there if it was the only way to protect Jessi and the girls.

"Fuck," he breathed.

He tightened his fingers anew around the bat. Took a step down. Listened. Forced a breath in and out of his lungs. Ground his teeth together when he felt they might start chattering.

He tried to make himself feel brave, but the emptiness in his chest and the black hole where his stomach used to be told the truth of how he really felt.

I won't let Victoria need that arrow, he told himself. I won't let it near her.

He took another step and listened again. Another tap and it sounded like thunder in the still of the night.

"I got something for you," he said, knowing, somehow, that it would here. "Come on, you fucker."

He got to the floor and his feet touched cold wood. He waited for it to tap again, giving away its location. A chill was in the air and David half-expected to see his breath when he exhaled. He looked to the right, into the living room, wondering if he'd see its silhouette outside the window.

The bat was raised, ready. He looked to the left, into the kitchen. He didn't see anything outside, no hulking shapes or burning red eyes.

Now that he was down here, it wasn't going to tap again. He would have to find it himself. He started with the living room, keeping the bat cocked over his shoulder. It might not kill a werewolf, but it would crack a skull, and if necessary he'd just keep bashing until the sun rose.

He crept close to the glass without getting right up next to it, peered outside. It looked clear out there, so he moved to the next window. A sweep of the living room revealed nothing. He went to the front door and looked out that window, but, again, there was nothing there. He considered turning on the porch light, hoping he could scare it away, but on the other hand, it might react differently. For all he knew, the light might cause it to attack.

In the kitchen, he stood in the middle of the room and swept all the windows from there. When he saw nothing waiting outside, he decided to move closer and make sure.

He realized his breathing had returned to something like normal, even though that pit in his stomach hadn't gone away. He recognized the feeling as anticipation. He tapped the glass with the tip of the bat and immediately regretted it.

Why would you tell it where you are, he thought. It's playing a smarter game than you and it's going to end badly for you if you don't wise up.

He went to the other windows but, just like the living room, he didn't see anything outside. He felt his fingers tingling and realized he was high on adrenaline. That was good, though; he would need it if the monster attacked.

It was toying with him, he decided. It was going to wait until he let his guard down. This was the point in the movie where the hero thinks he's finally safe, and that's when Jason jumps through the window in slow motion. He had seen too many movies to be taken by the ploy. He didn't turn his back to the windows and instead stood in the center of the kitchen, facing them, waiting and ready.

Two minutes passed in silence. Four minutes. Eight. Ten minutes. After fifteen, his feet couldn't take the cold of the kitchen floor anymore and he moved into the living room. He sat on the couch, eyes on the window, and waited.

He kept his ears tuned, but for all he could tell, the world outside was truly dead. Nothing moved out there. Maybe, he thought, it really had gone away.

Then he doubted his own memory. He thought he'd heard it scratching at the window, but had he? Maybe he'd been dreaming it when he woke up. Maybe the paranoia was getting to him. He expected to hear sounds in the night, so sounds in the night was what he heard. But had he really?

He thought about checking on Victoria, but if she hadn't heard anything and woken up, he didn't want to wake her now. Then again, he thought, if she *had* heard something and was lying awake terrified, he should comfort her.

He settled on a compromise. He turned on the kitchen light and started making himself a snack. If Victoria were awake, she would hear the noise, know he was up, and be reassured. Also, if something was outside, it might see him through the window, find him at ease, not worried at all, and back down. If he didn't show he was afraid, maybe the thing would leave him be after all.

It wasn't a flawless strategy, but it was all he had.

He made a turkey sandwich with hot mustard on toasted white bread, cut it diagonal, and sat on the couch, in the dark, to eat it. When the sandwich was gone, and David was still alive, he went back to put his plate in the sink and turn out the kitchen light.

Then he went back to the couch, lay the bat across his lap, and watched the windows for as long as he could keep his eyes open—which didn't turn out to be very much longer.

. . . .

DAVID TRIED TO CALL the Bewlays on his break that day at Cleo's Market, but they didn't answer. When he went to lunch, he tried again, but, still they didn't answer. He wanted to see if they could bring his knife by the house, drop it in the mailbox or something. He couldn't have it while on the clock at the store, but Jessi had kept the car, and he didn't want to tell her he had it just yet—or ever if he could avoid it. She hadn't laid eyes on that wedding set since they moved into their house, and if she ever did ask, he'd play dumb, and she'd believe him—so he couldn't drive by to pick it up after work.

He supposed he could wait until she picked him up, then, when they all got home, suddenly remember he was supposed to go by there for something.

He really needed another car. There was no chance of being able to pay to have his repaired, he'd just junk the thing and use the money to at least get a down payment on a new used something. This one car business was for the birds.

On his last break, he tried once more to call, and when they didn't answer, he left a message.

"Dude, it's me, where the fuck you at? I need to see if you guys got that knife ready for me? I need to come get it today if you do. Better yet, if you guys can slip it in my mailbox on the road without the wife seeing, you can stop by here—I'm at work, it's Saturday—and I'll buy you a whole case. But I really need it today, so one of you fuckers give me a call back. If I don't answer, I'm here until five, so just leave a message. Or text me. Something."

He hung up, made sure the phone was on vibrate in case they tried to call, then went back to stocking the dairy department. Every time he had to slide another gallon of milk into the rack, he thought of the smell of the thing outside his house.

When he got off that evening, he stopped in the bathroom after clocking out and checked his phone. Nothing from the Bewlays. Or anyone else, for that matter. Which led him to believe Jessi was either waiting for him outside, or almost here.

He tried one last time to get Mick or Donnie on the phone, again to no avail.

Fuckers, he thought. Lazy, shiftless bastards. If they don't have it ready tonight, I'm not buying them shit. I'll pay em for the labor and they can go buy their own fucking beer.

He slipped into his jacket and went outside.

He scanned the parking lot, but saw no sign of Jessi's car. He walked to the opposite end of the store and checked that end of the parking lot. Still nothing. He went back to where he came out, where she had dropped him off, telling himself to stay in one spot because if she showed up and didn't see him because he was wandering around, she might park and then he'd never find her.

After a while, she still hadn't shown and when he realized how long he'd been waiting, he looked at his phone.

Nothing on there from her indicating she would be late. Then he looked at the time and realized he'd been off work for half an hour.

He texted her, "I'm off," then waited for a reply. He scanned the parking lot again, wondering if he'd just missed her car somewhere, but he still didn't see her.

He watched the phone, trying to will a response. She wouldn't respond if she was driving—not with the girls in the car, anyway—so he tried to take the lack of response as a good thing. She was on her way. But there was a part of him that couldn't still that voice in the back of his head that told him she wasn't coming. She wasn't coming because she couldn't.

It was dark now, the moon was up, and the carnie had decided to torture David even more by killing his family and letting him live. He walked from one end of the parking lot to the other again, this time stopping at each row and looking for Jessi's car in an increasingly more frantic attempt to prove to himself that she and the girls were safe and sound. It would cause an argument if he'd been standing here for half an hour while she sat in the car waiting for him just a hundred feet away, but that was an argument he would gladly have if it meant everyone was okay.

Every second he stood here waiting felt like ten minutes, and five minutes felt like an hour. She hadn't returned his text. He tried to call, but after two rings, it went to voicemail.

"Fuck!" he said. "Answer your damned phone for a change, Jessi! That's why you have the fucking thing, so people can reach you when they need to!"

He thought about calling one of the girls' phones, but knew that, if he was just being paranoid and they really were on their way, he'd just look like a bigger doofus. Besides, he already felt enough like a child standing here waiting for his mommy to give him a ride.

He'd give them five more minutes.

They pulled into the parking lot three minutes later and the relief David felt rush into his heart made him think for a second the world was a happy place and all would be well. Jessi stopped in front of him and David slid into the passenger seat.

"You don't have to call," Jessi said. "I got your text, I knew you were off."

"You mean the text you didn't reply to?"

"Talk to your daughter," she replied. "She wanted to get into an argument right as I was getting ready to leave."

That means you can't reply and say I'll be there in a minute, he thought.

"About what," he said.

"She wants to spend the night at Brooke's house, and I told her no because it's late and Brooke lives just outside West on the other side and I'm not driving all that way tonight."

"Which one? Who's Brooke?"

"Victoria," Jessi said. "Some girl from school, I guess."

David shrugged. He was trying to see what the big deal was. Hell, he'd drive her, he didn't mind. But he knew that wasn't the response she was seeking and for all their minor bickering, David and Jessi had always maintained a united front when it came to the girls.

"She'll get over it," he said.

"So I had to spend however long it was standing there arguing with her and telling her she wasn't staying anywhere. I said if she wanted to stay from Friday to Sunday next weekend, that was fine, but she was too late tonight and anyway what good does it do going to someone's house to spend the night when it's already dark out and I still had to come pick you up?"

"God, I gotta look for a new car," David said, trying to get her mind off Victoria and the fight.

"You're not going to try to fix yours?"

He explained how it wasn't feasible and would make more sense to sell it for parts and use the money to get a new one instead.

"That makes sense," she said. "Have you started looking?"

"No, I was still undecided on what to do about it. But I'm gonna call Sandy in the morning and see what we can get for it. I'd like to have something by next weekend."

"Good," Jessi said. "We're wasting so much gas in this car, driving all over the place."

"I keep telling you to get me a job in the big leagues and we can ride together every day."

"We need a new janitor, if you're interested."

"Hmm."

When they got home, David went up to talk to Victoria and see how she was doing.

"I hear there was an argument," he said.

Victoria shrugged.

"How come it was so important to spend the night? You guys had some boys coming over?"

Victoria smiled and shook her head.

"No, dad!"

"Good. So what's up?"

She shrugged again.

He had a feeling he knew exactly what was wrong, but neither of them wanted to say it. He and Victoria had always had a certain bond. He often felt like they might resent him because he couldn't afford to spoil them like Jessi could, but on a personal level, he and Victoria were very close. So when he looked at her, he recognized the dread in her eyes, even if she didn't want to put a name to it.

And he knew why she felt that dread.

He wanted to hug her and tell her he wasn't going to let the monster get her, but acknowledging there was a monster at all wasn't exactly the way to reassure her.And since he hadn't been able to get hold of the Bewlays and collect his magic knife, he knew she would have seen through his brave face. Because David would die trying protect and defend his family, but the truth was he didn't know exactly what he was up against. He knew it could be vicious. He knew it was frigging big. And he knew it, in all likelihood, could tear him limb from limb if it got hold of him.

He pondered the idea of everyone staying at a motel in town for the night, just to wait out the carnival, but it was too late to think up an excuse for that.

"You never called animal control, did you?" she asked.

"I said I'd call, didn't I?" he said, knowing he was about to lie to his daughter, something he hated doing more than he hated anything. "They can't come get something that isn't there, though. They said animals are native to the area, but unless they're on the property, they can't do much about it."

"Did you tell them it was trying to get in?"

"Trying and getting in are two different things," David said, shrugging. "They were pretty much not helpful at all. But, there's one very important thing that makes humans better than animals."

"What's that?"

He held up his hand and wiggled the thumb.

"We can open doors."

The comment was meant to alleviate her concerns and make her think everything was fine.

"Nothing's gonna get in the house," he told her. "I promise."

And immediately he felt like a bastard for saying that, because there was absolutely no way he could assure that promise wasn't broken. He'd seen it, or at least the suggestion of it. If it wanted in, if it truly and finally wanted inside this house, there wasn't a lot David could do about it.

But the words seemed to please Victoria and for now making her feel better was the most important thing.

And as soon as he left her room, he went into the bathroom and tried to call Mick again.

"Dude, what the fuck?" he asked the voicemail. "Where you at? I need to come by and get that, if you're done with it, but I don't know if you are, so answer your damn phone and call me back."

He went downstairs and Jessi was making dinner, hamburgers from Cleo's Market cooked on the Foreman grill.

"Feeling better finally?" he asked and kissed the back of her head.

"Yeah," she said. "Little bit. Dinner'll be ready in ten minutes."

"Okay."

He went into the living room and stared into the dark outside the front window.

Where are you, motherfucker, he thought. Are you out there now? Are you watching me? He grabbed the baseball bat from beside the couch where it had, apparently, been all day, and held it up, showing the monster he was ready for it.

It was a shallow threat, he knew, but it was all he had right now.

He stood there until Jessi called him in for dinner. Afterward, the girls disappeared to their rooms and he and his wife watched a movie on television. He kept trying to get into it, but his attention was outside. And every time he'd try to focus on the story, he thought he heard something near the window. He sat there, with Jessi lying in his lap, his heart pounding with anticipation. The bat leaned against the side of the couch David sat against, within reach should he need it in an instant.

When the movie ended and Jessi got up and headed into the bathroom to get ready for bed, David pulled out his phone, saw he hadn't missed any calls or texts from Mick, and almost texted him asking where the hell they were.

Then he realized as late as it was, there was no way he could convince Jessi he needed to go over there right now, not without arousing some suspicion from his wife. But there was the added detail that doing so would leave Jessi and the girls alone in the dark.

It was simply too late. He had needed Mick and Donnie to come through for him and they hadn't. He just prayed that none of them would come to regret that in the morning.

Jessi came out of the bathroom and David went in. When he came out, he checked into the girls' rooms, kissed Allie goodnight, then went to Victoria's and did the same.

As he was closing the door, she was lying in bed on her phone still.

"Don't stay up too late," he said.

"I won't," she said and he knew she was lying. But he wasn't one to judge considering he'd told one of his own just a few hours earlier. Anyway, he knew she would be up late listening, waiting, worrying.

And he couldn't blame her. He knew he was in for a long night, too.

He got into bed, laying the bat on the floor next to him, and kissed Jessi goodnight.

"Why are you carrying that thing around?" she asked.

He shrugged and said, "Two people have been killed in their homes in the past week." That seemed to satisfy her and she turned over. David climbed in, then lay there staring at the window while she fell asleep.

He thought about the Bewlays and how often he had been there for them when they needed him. Okay, it wasn't often but that was because the Bewlays had always taken care of themselves, rarely asking for help. But if they did, he would be there no questions, and they knew it. And yet they couldn't do one simple thing for him when he had expressed several times his desperation for this. How clear did he have to be? Guys, I'm about ninety-nine percent sure one of the carnies is a werewolf and he's going to attack me, so I need a weapon made of silver that I can try to protect myself and my family with, can you please help me out?

He shouldn't have to resort to that, they should do it because they were his friends, he had asked them, and Mick had said okay. That should be all it took. And if they couldn't get it done today, then fucking tell him. They had a phone. They knew his number. How hard is it just to send a quick text?

"Sorry, no luck today, we'll finish tomorrow." Seven words, that's all it would have taken, and he would have been able to think of something else.

Instead, he spent the night like a lovelorn teen, waiting for a call that wasn't coming.

And it was with these thoughts in his head and a house filled with nothing but silence that, nearly an hour later, David actually dozed off.

He jumped awake some time later to a crash from downstairs. Jessi sat up, too, asking from her haze, "What was that?"

David knew, but didn't want to scare her, so he said, "I'll go see. Sounds like someone's in the house. You get the girls and hide, go out a window and get out of here if you can. Call the police when you get out."

He grabbed the bat and jumped out of bed and went to the door, knowing that to stall any longer would just enable it to take out its rage on his daughters. With that, he threw open the door and ran down the stairs.

He heard Jessi coming out of the room and padding to Allie's door.

David stopped at the bottom of the stairs, listening for where the werewolf was. He could smell it right away, and it was almost overpowering. He heard a growl from the living room and he raised the bat above his head and charged in. He saw the dark shape crouching in the shadows and brought the bat down hard on what he hoped was its skull. The metal rang off the bone like he'd hit concrete. It roared that stench into David's face, and David leapt back a few feet.

The thing stood up but as it rose and reached what he hoped was its full height, it just kept rising after that until it had to stand over seven feet tall. It was dark in the room, but he was able to make out enough of it to know what he was seeing.

He didn't want to believe it. He'd known what it was, but had still kept trying to tell himself that was insane, that there was another answer, that it was just a crazy man who thought he was a monster. But his heart had been right all along, and that reality chilled him to his core.

It bared its teeth and David swung again, this time connecting with its jaw, but when it brought its head back, it didn't seem at all fazed.

"Fuck," David muttered before bringing the bat up again. But before he could take another swing, the werewolf swiped at the bat, knocked it from David's hands, and it hit the opposite wall with a clang and a thud on the floor.

It took a step toward him and David dove across the room, out of the way and toward where he thought the bat had landed. It wasn't going to kill, or even hurt, the monster, but hopefully he could at least keep it distracted long enough for Jessi and the girls to get out.

The werewolf watched him move, taking its time, knowing it had the advantage.

It was playing with its food.

He found the bat and picked it up just as the monster tried to bat him aside, but he swung around and instead of connecting with David's body, the claws hit the bat. It lunged with its open maw, but David brought the end of the bat up into its jaw, knocking its head aside. Before it could come back from the blow, he swung again, this time into its temple. The werewolf showed pain for the first time and David took the moment to get back to his feet. He hit it again in the head, hoping to smash its skull, or at least blind it. Smash its snout. Break its teeth. Something. Anything.

It roared again and David felt all the air rushing out of his body. This thing wants to kill and eat me, he thought. Me, of all the people in the world, I'm the one it wants. And why? Because it happened upon me on the road?

What made him so special as to be its target?

He pulled back to swing again, and when he did it looked at him with red, angry eyes and opened its mouth wide, roaring into his face with a rage he'd never imagined before. The sight terrified him anew and all the bravado he was building up from hurting it suddenly vanished in a flash, leaving him feeling empty and defeated. He felt like he wouldn't even be able to lift the bat again.

It took a step in his direction, then stopped. David heard something, a THWIP sound he knew he'd heard before but couldn't place.

The werewolf took another step, leaving only a couple of feet between them. He tightened his fist around the bat, tried to lift it but all the strength had left his arms.

Another THWIP and the werewolf was jolted in its place. It turned around and David saw in its silhouette two long black lines issuing from its body in the front and back. He wasn't so far in shock that he didn't recognize what they were.

He looked to the left and saw her in the doorway. Victoria already had a third arrow nocked. She released and it flew into the wolf's chest, this time causing it to howl. Blood spurted from its chest in rhythm to the beating of its heart.

David swung the bat at the back of its knees and the wolf folded to the floor. He ripped the arrow from its chest and slammed it into the thing's eye, trying to penetrate to the brain, forcing the shaft further into the hole, deeper into the skull.

The beast tried to claw at him and Victoria shot an arrow through its hand, into its torso, pinning it in place.

David stood up and moved back, looking down at his handiwork. The werewolf didn't move, but he could still hear it breathing.

"Is it going to die?" Victoria asked.

"I don't know," David admitted. The arrows weren't tipped in silver. But it had lost a lot of blood.

"Is it's heart still in the same place?"

He shrugged and said, "I guess. I really have no idea."

She fired an arrow straight into its heart and the werewolf gave one weak grunt, then died.

David and Victoria moved back to the doorway, in case it had a final jump scare in it somewhere.

"Did your mother call the police?"

Victoria nodded and said, "Uh huh."

"She was supposed to get you guys out of here."

"She fought me," Victoria said. "I kind of knocked her out."

Shocked, David looked down at his daughter.

"You did *what*?"

"She wouldn't let me help, so I knocked her over the head with a book, like you see in movies."

"Christ, that actually works?"

"Apparently."

"You're going to be grounded for so long for that."

"I'll take it," she said. "Beats being dead."

"That it does."

Within minutes, the lights and sirens were outside, coming up the Old Back Road, pulling into David's driveway. Engines died and feet were heard outside. By then, David had already turned on the light and sat on the couch. They found him staring at the dead body and crying.

Mick lay bloody, naked and mangled on the living room floor.

• • • •

DAVID CALLED INTO WORK that day. It was almost 9:00 and David saw Officer Cline's car coming up the drive. He'd been standing at the window most of the morning, trying to reconcile what he'd seen with what he knew about life. Or what he thought he knew.

He told himself he was still in shock. How could it be Mick Bewlay? He'd known the brothers most of his life. He'd spent the night at their house. He'd never suspected anything like this before. What had happened? And did Donnie know about it?

He opened the door for the cop before Officer Cline had even walked up the porch.

Cline, whom David had gone to school with also, and whom he remembered not caring for at the time, nodded in thanks and stepped inside.

"So," he said, taking off his hat. "We found something at the Bewlay place we thought you might like to know."

"What?" David asked. He looked around the house, hoping Jessi and the girls weren't around. They'd all spent most of the morning upstairs, still scared at what had happened and mostly stunned into silence. Before Officer Cline could tell him, David felt dread rising and he wondered if he wanted to hear this at all.

"We found a basement."

David frowned.

"Basement? In a trailer?"

"Yeah," Officer Cline said, "that's what we thought. Apparently they had dug it out, with a trapdoor under the carpet in the hall."

"Alright," David said, confused and curious now.

"In the basement—not really a *basement* basement, more like a root cellar—we found a cage. Inside it was the mauled remains of an unidentified male. Off the record, Mr. Reed, we think it might be Donnie Bewlay."

"Fuck," David said as all the air left his body. That explained why every time he'd called in the last week, Mick told him Donnie was out. "Are you sure?"

Cline shrugged and said, "Nothing official without an examination, this is off the record, one Indian to another." Indians were the mascot at the high school where David taught, and where he'd met Timmy Cline back in the day. "But, yeah, I'd put my money on it."

"Wow. That's...I don't even know."

"Yeah," Cline nodded. "Crazy stuff in this town."

David wanted to roll his eyes and tell Tim Cline that there was nothing crazy in Green Lake, that one werewolf does not automatically make Green Lake a happening town. Instead he just nodded and said, "Thanks for telling me. Off the record. Hey," he lowered his voice a little just in case Jessi could hear, "did you find any silverware, in a box or something? I dropped some off to them the other day and I was hoping I could get it back."

Cline looked up at the ceiling, searching his memory up there, and said, "I don't remember. Sorry."

"That's okay, thanks," David said.

Cline hung around a bit, asking a few more questions, the same questions David had already answered a few hours ago, "just to make sure we've got all the facts straight," Cline said, then he finally left and David resumed standing at the window and trying to come to terms with this new world he found himself in where myths walked the earth.

• • • •

HE TOOK JESSI'S CAR later under the pretense of getting some money from Sandy Miller for the sale of David's car as junk. It wasn't much, he said, but would work as a down payment on something else.

This wasn't a lie; he had talked to Sandy briefly, saying, "Whatever you can pay for it, whatever's it worth, man; I just want to get it off my hands."

But it was only an excuse to get out of the house. He had to drive by the Bewlay place.

He didn't want to, of course. What he wanted to do was scrub the memory of them from his brain and then, maybe, eventually, he'd be able to sleep again, which he was pretty sure he wouldn't be doing for a while now.

Sandy handed him $500 and David stuffed it into his wallet thinking about another small lie he'd told. This would be a down payment on another *used* car. And most likely a cheap one, at that. But it would get him where he was going.

He would look in the paper and online tomorrow for a car. Right now he had other things to do.

He drove out toward the Bewlay property, expecting police guards and roadblocks to turn him away, but they must have done all they needed to for the day because the place was deserted.

Still, he didn't pull up to the place, but parked back a bit and walked. The crime scene tape had been strung around the house, but David stepped past it, then stopped and stared at the trailer.

He thought again how impossible all this was. To think his closest friend in the world had this secret. And how long had he been carrying it? Surely not his whole life. David would have seen it.

And on that note, if Mick was such a good friend, why had he been stalking David? Why attack him? David would never have hurt Mick if not for this.

Maybe because David knew him? Maybe the wolf part of him wanted to eliminate any potential threats to being found out. Maybe that's why Donnie had been killed?

Or maybe Donnie was just bad luck, wrong place at the wrong time when his brother had turned.

But why did they have a cage under the trailer?

The windows of the trailer hung in the air, black and uninviting.

David stepped around to the side of the building, toward the porch. He was trying to see, but he'd waited too long to find his excuse today and the sun was already setting. He walked closer, slowly, cautiously, trying to peer into the dark, and then he spied it, under the firewood where he'd left it.

The fucker hadn't even touched the silverware. This made David think Mick had known exactly what he was and what was going to happen. Until now, he kept trying to tell himself that it hadn't been Mick, that Mick wouldn't attack David or his family like that. But the silverware resting right where he'd left it, with no sign of Mick even attempting to do as David had asked spoke volumes.

He picked up the box and the wood clattered to the porch with a rattle that made David's bones ache in the stillness.

He was halfway back to the car when he heard a whisper from the woods.

He almost dropped the box and took off running, but there was something familiar in the sound. He stopped and looked around, but it was too dark to see. He waited, wondering if he'd imagined it. Then it came again.

"Dave," in a hoarse whisper, to his right.

He looked over and saw nothing but dark woods.

"Dave!" it came again. He turned toward the woods, trying like hell to see in there.

Finally, he saw a black mass move among the rest of the dark and he had that urge again to take off running. Mick's ghost was here, ready to finish the job. That's when he recognized it wasn't Mick, but Donnie.

"What the fuck!" he said out loud. "Donnie, where the fuck you been? Man, the cops are going to want to talk to you, I thought you were dead."

David was walking toward him through the brush and when they met, he couldn't believe his eyes.

"Dude, what the hell is going on? Do you know what your brother did?"

Donnie nodded and said, "Yeah, man. I'm sorry. I didn't know he was going to go after you."

"You knew about ... what he was?"

Donnie nodded again. "For a while now. But we had it taken care of. There's a cage—"

"Under the house, yeah, the cops told me," David said. "But they told me they found your remains down there."

Donnie frowned and said, "Remains? I'm right here."

"Man, I know. But they said there was a mangled up body down there and they thought it was you."

"No, not me. And I have no idea who it was. Shit, that's not good."

"None of this is good. What the holy hell happened?"

"I don't know for sure," Donnie said. He seemed either out of breath or terrified. "We found something in the woods a couple months back, this wooden box. It was buried near where we were digging to put a new still."

"Just make the shit in your kitchen, man, it's not against the law here."

""I know I know," Donnie said. "Anyway, we found this box. Mick brought it home. I don't know what it was, we never did figure it out. But then the dreams started. Weird shit, about running and killing, about eating. Before the month was up, Mick said we needed to dig the hole for protection. And it turned out he was right."

"You dug that hole to keep him locked up?"

Donnie nodded.

"How'd that work out?"

"Worked fine at first. I went down there earlier, after I saw the cops leave. The chain was broken, that's all I can figure."

"Where the hell were you? I've been talking to Mick every day this week almost. Were you even here?"

"No," Donnie said. "That's my fault. I told him I needed to take off for a few days, just get my head together, you know? I thought a few days in the woods might do me some good."

"But when it happened, you weren't here to make sure he didn't get out?"

Donnie looked at the ground and shook his head slowly from side to side.

"I'm sorry," he said. "I didn't think he would ever go after you."

David shrugged.

"This is still all just too crazy. I can barely even process this. First thing you need to do, though, is get rid of that fucking box. If that's what caused this, it needed to be gone, like yesterday."

"Already done. That's where I've been. I was just coming back when I saw your car out here and decided to wait for you."

"You need to call the cops. Tell them what happened."

"Yeah yeah," Donnie said. He was nervous, David could tell. He kept looking around, as if he expected an ambush. These two never did care much for authority. As much as Donnie knew it was the thing to do, David knew calling the cops was right under razorblade enema on Donnie's list of priorities.

"Yeah," he repeated a third time. "I need to, it's just ... I know. S'just that ..."

"What?" David asked, feeling the weight of the box of silverware in his arms finally. "What's up? Shit, did you hurt yourself? We need to get you to the hospital?"

David had noticed Donnie was bleeding. A trickle of it ran down from somewhere in his scalp, down his jaw to his neck.

Donnie wiped at the blood and said, "I'm alright, it'll be okay."

"What did you do?"

As he looked, the flow not only continued, but got stronger until it wasn't just dripping down his face, but running, then gushing.

"I'll be fine," Donnie croaked. "I just gotta ... just ... it's just, I—"

"What the fuck, dude?"

"It's just ... I gotta eat."

Donnie's head split open and he clawed at the frayed skin, ripping, pulling it down, skinning himself like a deer, but what he revealed under the flesh wasn't the inside of Donnie Bewlay. David heard the crack and snap of bones and from the top of Donnie's head emerged a wolf, snout first, birthing itself as Donnie's body folded to the ground.

Before its head was even out, it was snarling and snapping at David.

"Holy fucking shit!" he screamed, dropping the box of silverware.

It fell open, spilling its contents in a loud CLANG of metal on metal.

He stared in shock at the wolf emerging from his friend. He wondered if maybe Victoria might have left a stray arrow in Jessi's car at some point. They'd done the job against Mick, after all, leaving the myth of needing silver to kill a werewolf officially busted, he thought.

Then he realized that, while he may not need silver, he had some handy, at his feet. He looked at the mess of tangled flatware and dropped to the ground, fishing blindly with his hands in the mess while his eyes remained glued to the monster before him.

His hands closed around useless spoons, ineffectual forks and dull butter knives. Then something jabbed him and he looked down to see something he didn't recognize as anything he'd used before. It looked like a cross between a knife and a beveled spatula, like something used to serve cake. The tip was sharp and the whole thing was no wider than a standard butter knife.

He looked at it, looked at the wolf, then clutched it tightly in his fist and leapt, driving the blade deep into its eye socket before it could gain any purchase outside Donnie's body.

As soon as he felt it hit something inside, he jumped back and dug the keys from his pocket. If it came after him, he'd jump in the car. But as he watched it, he didn't think it was going to chase him. It flailed around on the ground, ripping its arms free as it sloughed off more of Donnie Bewlay.

It fell onto its back, stretching, arching, reaching for the moon as it cried in pain.

This wasn't the reaction David had expected. Maybe one didn't *need* silver, but maybe silver did a better job anyway. This was certainly more dramatic than what had happened to Mick.

He felt sick at the sight before him. Blood gushed and meat hung in loose flaps as the thing struggled to get free, all the while trying not to die.

David considered stabbing its other eye with a silver fork, but was afraid it would scratch him. Wasn't that the rule, too? A scratch or a bite from a werewolf turned you into one?

He kept his distance and watched.

Eventually, the thing gave up struggling and lay there, still only partially released from Donnie's limp skin, which hung off the wolf like a dirty suit.

It lay there, panting, trying to breathe. It whined and David felt almost sorry for it.

Its arms spasmed, then went still.

It made one final effort to growl, but what came from its mouth sounded more like surrender. With that, it died in the dirt with the moon reflecting off its slick skin.

David gathered the rest of the flatware and tossed it into the car. Then he went back and looked at the mess. He didn't want to do it, but there was no way around it. He leaned down and yanked the knife out of its eye, then hurried back to the car before it could miraculously come back to life and gut him.

He pulled away from the Bewlay farm and didn't look back. As he made his way home in the dark, he saw silhouetted in the distance, the small black shapes of the carnival dismantling before moving on.

END

THANK YOU FOR READING this book. I hope you will consider leaving an honest review.

• • • •

IF YOU WOULD LIKE TO keep up to date on my writing and where it can be found, why not join my FREE weekly newsletter HERE[1].

---

1. https://cdennismoore.us3.list-manage.com/

subscribe?u=98166cbe6a6ccf1d7a39e772e&id=ac9e73819c

Don't miss out!

Visit the website below and you can sign up to receive emails whenever C. Dennis Moore publishes a new book. There's no charge and no obligation.

https://books2read.com/r/B-A-EPXB-DVTG

BOOKS 2 READ

Connecting independent readers to independent writers.

Did you love *The Werewolves of Green Lake*? Then you should read *The Vampires of Green Lake*[2] by C. Dennis Moore!

[3]

The werewolves were dead and David Reed just wanted life for his family to return to normal. But a mysterious wooden box found in the woods suggests that word has a whole new meaning, one he's not prepared for. As he tries to uncover the secrets of the box, a new threat emerges from the night, and it's targeting those closest to him. David has to unlock the mystery of the box in order to uncover the face in the darkness and the source of those horrible sounds coming from down the hall.

---

2. https://books2read.com/u/mV7B8A

3. https://books2read.com/u/mV7B8A

What will he do when the vampires come calling on Green
Lake?

About the Author

C. Dennis Moore is the author of the Angel Hill novels, the Monsters of Green Lake series, as well as the Holiday Horrors. He lives in St. Joseph, MO with his wife, Kara. They have seven children and three grandchildren.